Keely, **Emma** and **Tahlia** work together
at a small, trendy design company in Melbourne.
They've become the best of friends, meeting for
breakfast, chatting over a mid-morning coffee
and a doughnut—or going for a cocktail after work.
They've loved being single in the city…but now
three gorgeous new men are about to enter their work
lives, transform their love lives—and give them
loads more to gossip about!

Don't miss each story in this great new trilogy
brought to you by Mills & Boon® Tender Romance™!

Office Gossip
*From sexy bosses to surprise babies—
these girls have got everyone talking!*

Last month, September 2005:
Impossibly Pregnant by Nicola Marsh
A positive pregnancy test is a surprise for Keely!

This month, October 2005:
The Shock Engagement by Ally Blake
Emma has always dreamed of marrying Harry.
Now they're engaged—but it's all a sham.
Will he ever be hers for real…?

The month after next, November 2005:
Taking on the Boss by Darcy Maguire
Tahlia's furious that the promotion she's been
working so hard for has been given to someone else!
He's now her new boss—and he's *gorgeous*!

Having once been a professional cheerleader, **Ally Blake** believes in the motto 'Smile and the world smiles with you'. One way to make Ally smile is by sending her on holidays, especially to locations which inspire her writing. New York and Italy are by far her favourite destinations. Other things that make her smile are the gracious city of Melbourne, the gritty Collingwood football team, and her gorgeous husband Mark. Reading romance novels is a smile-worthy pursuit from long back, so, with such valuable preparation already behind her, she wrote and sold her first book. Her career as a writer also gives her a perfectly reasonable excuse to indulge in her stationery addiction. That alone is enough to keep her grinning every day! Ally would love you to visit her at her website www.allyblake.com

Recent titles by the same author:

THE WEDDING WISH
MARRIAGE MATERIAL
MARRIAGE MAKE-OVER
HOW TO MARRY A BILLIONAIRE
A MOTHER FOR HIS DAUGHTER

THE SHOCK ENGAGEMENT

BY
ALLY BLAKE

MILLS & BOON®

To all of the fabulous women I have ever worked
alongside—especially the Sussie Chadrock superstars
for their endless enthusiasm.

*First published in Great Britain 2005
Harlequin Mills & Boon Limited,
Eton House, 18-24 Paradise Road, Richmond, Surrey TW9 1SR*

© Ally Blake 2005

ISBN 0 263 18734 9

*Set in Times Roman 10½ on 12¼ pt.
07-0805-50140*

*Printed and bound in Great Britain
by Antony Rowe Ltd, Chippenham, Wiltshire*

CHAPTER ONE

*GIRLS' NIGHT IN WITH **WHEN HARRY MET SALLY***
*'Ha! Try telling my Harry that men and women can't be
friends!' Emma said, throwing popcorn at the TV.*

THEIR eyes met across the crowded room.
*Emma's gaze drank in dark brown sun-kissed hair, an
outback tan, a strong straight nose, a three-day stubble and
clear hazel eyes dancing with mischief. When the man
across the room smiled at her, her knees, ankles and elbows
all turned to jelly.*

Thunk! That was the sound of Emma's elbow slipping
off her office desk. When her chin nearly followed in its
wake she was jolted from her daydream. Her fuzzy gaze
cleared to find a field of stars swimming across her computer
monitor. With a great sniff she sat up straight and shuffled
her mouse to bring her work back upon the screen.

Prior to disappearing into her terribly nice daydream,
Emma had been working on the animation portion of *Flirt*
magazine's Australia's Hunkiest Bloke competition project.
After creating a whiz-bang website for *Flirt* magazine,
WWW Designs had been called upon to produce a dynamic
presentation for the big awards night that Saturday. The
problem was the page Emma was working on was half pho-
tograph and half bio of one of the nominees and, you
guessed it—he had hazel eyes, an outback tan and a smile
that turned her to jelly!

The bachelor in question was Harry Buchanan, the creator

of *Harold's House*—a hugely successful Internet browser created expressly for kids—and he was also her very best friend in the whole world. Adding to the distraction factor, she had been secretly in love with the guy her whole adult life and that afternoon he was due to arrive in Melbourne for his yearly visit. It was enough to have a girl indulging in daydreams all day.

Emma's focus shifted and she caught her reflection in the monitor. With her newly chopped blonde bob with its blunt fringe and shimmering highlights, she seemed so pale compared with Harry's healthy complexion, and where unrestrained sexual energy sizzled in Harry's eyes she was so obviously a wide-eyed innocent.

She looked closer. Ick! That day she was more red-eyed than wide-eyed. Unable to sleep from excitement the night before, she had searched her astounding collection of DVDs for an antidote. Staying up until one in the morning watching *Love Story* had probably not been the best choice as no amount of white eyeliner had been able to hide the evidence.

Determined to snap back into the real world and forget about Harry until he actually arrived, she closed the offending page and opened up her Blondie file. Blondie was the skinny little cartoon girl with a cute blonde ponytail and big blue eyes she had created to host the competition on the *Flirt* website and who would make an appearance on the awards night. Blondie simpered and giggled and pointed and fainted like a master in the bottom corner of the screen every time a new hunky bachelor was revealed.

Happy that Blondie was as endearing as she would ever be, Emma ran off a print copy of the animated girl's various stunts and expressions, stuffed it into a pink folder and hot-footed towards the stationery room to make copies for the demonstration they would give *Flirt*'s people the next day.

Of course a quick stop in the kitchenette for a fortifying coffee and cookie could not be avoided.

Pouring herself an oversized double Espresso, she hummed the theme to *Love Story* under her breath as she waited. Damn it! Now she would be humming it all day!

Suddenly her boss, a prickly, sharp-minded woman known affectionately as Rabid Raquel, stormed into the room.

'You can't pull that crap with me!' Raquel screeched at some hapless guy down the mobile phone clamped to her ear. She opened the fridge and stared into it as though looking for the answers to her problems within. Emma tucked herself back into the corner of the room, quietly sipping on her coffee, doing her dandiest not to get caught in the indiscriminate spray of her boss's wrath.

'Fix it. Now! Or it'll be your head!' Raquel snapped the phone shut, slammed the fridge door and only then seemed to notice Emma was there.

'Ms Radfield. I assume your little cartoon is ready for the final *Flirt* magazine meeting tomorrow.'

Emma flapped the pink folder at her boss. 'All ready. No worries.'

'Because this has to be perfect,' Raquel insisted. 'Nothing can go wrong. *Nothing*.'

Emma noticed a light sheen of sweat had taken up residence on Raquel's brow. Raquel did mean for a living, but this was different. She was worried.

'Raquel, it's perfect,' Emma promised, her voice soft, calming, sure. 'Everyone has done a great job on this campaign. *Flirt* will love it to bits.'

Raquel's steely glare meant she didn't believe a word of it, but Emma knew better than to push her luck. She would have the presentation ready in time as she promised and that would have to be enough.

'Would you like to see a copy?' Emma asked.

Raquel fluffed a hand in front of her face as though swatting away a persistent fly. 'No! Too, too busy. Just consider it a priority. You never know, you might need *Flirt* magazine for a reference. Some day...' Raquel disappeared out the door, marched down the hallway and was lost within the crowd before Emma could even blink.

What was that all about? A reference? Some day?

Before she had time to absorb Raquel's odd threat, Emma's mobile beeped and she flinched.

She clicked the right buttons to bring up the message. It was from Tahlia, her best mate and WWW's sales guru.

em, is australia's hunkiest bloke there yet?

Emma's mouth kicked up at one corner. A right twenty-first century girl, she managed to type a message with one hand, sip her coffee with the other and walk the crowded office hallway towards the stationery room without making one typo or spilling a drop.

not yet T & don't mention it to him or he'll get an even bigger head

Within seconds her phone buzzed and beeped.

didn't know you liked guys with big heads...

Emma shot back a final text message.

watch yourself or i'll come down there and bop you on the head with that industrial sized stapler you are so in love with

Now, having given in and progressed to whistling the theme to *Love Story* loud and proud, Emma skipped into the stationery room to find Raquel's assistant, Penelope, head down, hunched over a photocopier in the far corner.

'Morning, Penny!' Emma called out.

Penelope spun around, her hand to her heart, her eyes large and bright. She then grabbed her bunch of papers and ran from the room like a startled rabbit. Emma shook her head. Poor duffer. Working so closely with Raquel would be enough to turn any sane woman into one big raw nerve.

Emma headed for the photocopier Penelope had been using, figuring it would save her time trying to find one that was working *and* stocked with A4 paper. She lifted the lid to find a sheet face down in place already. She turned back to the door, but Penelope was long gone.

Checking to see if it was anything important or whether she should just toss it away, Emma read the first few lines of the letter in her hand. That was all it took for her to realise just how important the document was.

'Oh, my.' Emma's hand covered her mouth as she devoured the gist of the letter. It was from Raquel's lawyers. WWW Designs was being sued. For a lot of money. Gossip about trouble had been whispered up and down the corridors for weeks, and now Emma knew why.

Raquel was dedicated and driven but excessively so. She had a thing for 'special assignments'. She encouraged her worker bees to go out of their way to know all there was to know about prospective clients in order to land said clients. She called it PR, her worker bees called it slave-driving. But it worked. For the most part, it worked. Keely, the other musketeer in Emma's trio of workmates and the web design genius of the crew, had in fact met her darling fiancé Lachlan, on such a 'special assignment'.

But since then there had been one infamous time it hadn't worked. Raquel had lobbied hard for the privilege to design and manage the personal website of a media magnate. She had sent one of her lapdogs to follow the guy around and in the process the lapdog had delved deep enough to discover that the magnate had a mistress. His wife had found out, had filed for divorce and now the magnate was suing, for big bucks, and Raquel was caught in the thick of it.

'Oh, my, oh, my, oh, my,' Emma whispered aloud.

The rumours, Raquel's throwaway line about needing a reference, the niggling bad feeling Tahlia'd had for some time, were all true. No wonder poor Penelope had looked fit to explode on the spot. She knew how bad it all was.

Needing to sit and think, Emma gave up on the idea of photocopying anything. She slipped the offending letter into her pink folder and rushed back towards her office. She threw her half-empty coffee cup into a nearby rubbish bin, tucked her phone back on to her belt, popped a mint into her mouth and rounded the corner towards her office.

'Emma, wait!' Chrystal, WWW Designs' busty receptionist, skipped alongside Emma, her red curls bouncing and red lips shining. 'You have a visitor. I showed him into your office. Hope you don't mind. Though you could have done a girl a favour and taken your time in coming back.' Chrystal kissed her fingers. *'Magnifico!'*

Emma stared back at Chrystal, searching the minefield of scattered thoughts of lawsuits and threats and panic for a way to decipher Chrystal's words. And then a voice from the past, a voice rich with experience and humour, the voice that had been echoing in her head and keeping her from real work all day, said from deep within her office, 'That can't possibly be little Emma Radfield, can it?'

Emma looked up to find six feet of heaven in a battered leather jacket and low-slung jeans leaning against her desk. 'Harry!'

'Come here, you luscious length of woman, you.'

She didn't need to be told twice. She threw her pink folder on to a nearby chair and leapt into Harry's waiting arms, grabbing fists full of the back of his ancient caramel-coloured jacket, her cheek rubbing against the supple collar, giddily breathing in the familiar scent—fresh air and sunshine mixed with something decidedly male, decidedly Harry.

'You're early!' she noted, but she was so happy to see him she could barely stop grinning.

He held her at arm's length, his hands keeping a gentle grip on her shoulders. 'And you're different,' he said.

Understatement of the year, Emma thought, but she bit her lip and let him play his game.

He twirled her back and forth, held her wrist to his ear to check her pulse and shook her a little as though trying to place the change. 'What could it be?' he asked. 'I just can't put my finger on it.'

Hair that has been waist-length for ever now chopped into a slick bob? The last remains of my puppy-fat gone by way of power Pilates? Usual tomboy uniform of jeans and T-shirt replaced with a black suit that looks as though it has been sewn on? All somewhat proving that I am anybody but little *Emma Radfield.*

'Nope,' he finally said. 'Must have been a trick of the light.'

Oh, he'd noticed, all right. Emma could see it in the barely there furrow of his brow. Though she could tell he didn't quite know what to make of it yet, he *had* noticed.

'So how are you?' she asked with a bright smile. 'Mr big time CEO. I didn't know if you would come this year now that you are such a busy big shot.'

'Aw, shucks,' he said. 'You know me. Gracious. Benevolent. Giving of my precious time.'

'Not so giving of your precious time that you could make it to my surprise birthday party.'

Harry winced. Bullseye!

'I tried, babes. Really I did. But…circumstances kept me away. Yet here I am now, as always, choosing to spend all the free time I can wangle with you.'

'As opposed to…?'

'Basking on the beaches of Acapulco, getting to know the local girls—'

'Oh, diddums. Life's tough.'

'You have no idea,' he said, smiling, but Emma knew there was a kernel of truth to the words. He wasn't yet thirty and yet with *Harold's House* he had created a modern day marvel, a masterpiece, a powerhouse. Now the question on everyone's lips in the Internet biz was: what was Wonder Boy Buchanan going to do next? It was a hard act to follow, especially for the man himself.

'And you also have no idea how much I missed you, kiddo,' he said, smiling into her eyes.

'Me too, Harry,' Emma said, her throat closing up.

With a thick growl, Harry once again took her in a great bear hug, lifting her off the ground as if she was a doll, not five-foot-six of digital animator who enjoyed a daily white chocolate macadamia cookie as much as the next girl.

Emma revelled in the feeling of swinging through the air as he twirled her about. That was until her flailing legs caught a hold of the edge of her office chair, sending it crashing to the ground in a mess of screeching metal and spinning wheels.

Her office door crashed open and a familiar face peered in. 'What on earth is going on in here?' Keely asked, her eyes twinkling.

Emma fought back a laugh. Keely was six months pregnant, which was a happy little miracle, but it was also making her more forgetful as the months progressed. Always one to tuck a pen behind her ear, her hairdo now had several pens tucked into and about it. She was a walking stationery case. Keely folded her slim arms atop her slightly rounded tummy.

Emma scrambled out of Harry's arms and straightened her twisted black trouser suit. Harry hid behind her as much as a guy double her size could. Emma shot daggers at Keely with her eyes, waiting until the sound of the spinning wheels of the office chair slowed and stopped.

'Um, Harry, this is Keely Rhodes. Keely, this is Harry Buchanan.'

Keely's face said *duh* as her lips said, 'Nice to meet you, Harry.'

Emma only hoped that Harry was not so understanding as to what Keely's expression gave away—that Emma had been a basket case all day—well, all week really, awaiting his arrival. Emma pulled away from Harry and moved to push her nosey friend back out the door.

'You promised to let us know as soon as he arrived,' Keely whispered through clenched teeth as she jabbed a finger at her silent mobile phone. 'A quick text message would have been fine. You didn't need to break any furniture in a fit of passion.'

Emma glanced over to Harry but he was blithely oblivious to their conversation as he picked up the heavy chair with one hand and tucked it under her desk.

'Though I have to say; now I totally get your years of pining. He's swoon-worthy, Em.'

'And you're engaged,' Emma reminded her.

'Engaged, yes. But blind to the allure of a hot guy? Never!'

'Get out now,' Emma quietly demanded.

Good deed done, Harry followed them to the door and reached around Emma to shake Keely's hand. 'It *is* a pleasure to finally meet you, Keely.'

Emma groaned inwardly as Keely gave Harry a detailed once-over, taking in his too-long hair, weather-beaten jacket, jeans with the knees almost worn away and scuffed boots, all which did little to cover the fact that this was one superb specimen of Australian manhood.

'I assure you, Harry,' Keely purred, 'the pleasure is all mine.'

Having borne the brunt of such obvious female attention ever since Emma had known him, Harry just grinned, generating his lady-killer smile, guaranteed to melt a pair of female knees at fifty paces. He then tucked himself in behind Emma once more, resting a casual hand across her hip, and Emma had to stop herself from leaping away from his feather-light touch. She had long since learned to control her instincts when it came to Harry's effortless, yet entirely innocent, caresses.

He rested his chin on her shoulder. She could feel his warm breath tickling at her ear. 'So are you two partners in crime?' he asked. 'Sharing secrets and lipstick? Shopping together for sexy underwear—'

Emma gave Harry an abrupt elbow in the ribs and was rewarded with a hearty 'Oomph' from his direction.

'You'll find it's best to ignore him, Keely.'

'It's called charm,' Harry murmured against her ear.

'It's called pathological. I know it's not yet five, Keely, but can you cover for me if I take off a tad early?'

Keely grinned and winked. 'I'll tell the Rabid Rottweiler you are out buying a new paintbrush or something. So go, take this man of yours home.'

'You heard the lady, Em,' Harry said. 'Let's blow this joint.'

'See ya,' Keely said and Emma looked up in time to see Harry throwing her a wink as she slipped out the door.

'She's engaged, lover boy.'

'Meaning she's not married,' he said, his eyes bright and laughing.

'Yet quite obviously with child.' Emma reached around to pinch him on the arm, using the brief respite to slip out of his embrace. She backed Harry towards her desk so she could tidy up her gear for the day.

Pens were in their holders. Papers were neat. Emails had all been answered. She still had to photocopy the Blondie files for the *Flirt* presentation but that could wait.

'Em, I can come back later if you have to finish up here,' Harry offered.

She shook her head. For once she could put others on the back burner for a day. Especially since seeing Harry in the flesh was almost enough to fry her brain of all other information. Almost. Her seriously disturbing discoveries of that morning were still playing at the back of her mind. Her finger rolled over her mouse as she considered sending off a quick heads-up to Tahlia and Keely.

But it was no use worrying her friends. Not until she had more information and not until she had done what she could to fix the situation first. She had long since proven to herself she could shoulder worry enough for everyone.

'Earth to Emma!'

She blinked and shook her head. 'Sorry, Harry. I'm coming.' She tucked her hair behind her ear and looked up to find Harry leaning in the doorway, his arms folded across his chest, watching her with a funny little smile.

With his scruffy sun-kissed brown hair and his crinkly hazel eyes that made a person smile just by looking at them, he was just so categorically gorgeous she had to fight back a sigh.

She shut down her computer, grabbed her briefcase, slipping the pink folder inside, and wandered back to Harry's side like a homing pigeon returning to its master. He wrapped an arm about her neck, all but strangling her as he dragged her from the office and through the hallway towards the lift.

'Come on,' he said. 'All these walls are making me antsy.'

'You've been inside ten minutes at most.'

His grip loosened enough so that he could look down into her face. 'Mmm,' he said, his voice a distant rumble. 'Too long.'

Something in his tone made her wonder if he was talking about his drought of sunshine or his year away from her side. Either way, it was good to see him too.

Emma hustled Harry to the lift. She knew by the disturbance of sighs following in her wake that Harry was bestowing grins all around.

Gracious? Benevolent? Giving of his precious time? Yeah, right! She knew that he would be lapping up the fact that he was likely receiving those smiles back in kind from her many young female co-workers.

Once at the lift, she pressed the down button and was surprised when the double doors gave way instantly. But when she saw Tahlia inside the lift hastily fixing her hair and smoothing out her clothes, she knew that her other best buddy had been summoned by Keely.

Emma crossed her arms. 'What a surprise to see you down here.'

Tahlia looked up, her cheeks glowing pink. 'Oh. Well, I borrowed Keely's industrial sized stapler,' she said, waving it in Emma's face as proof, 'and she emailed to say she needed it. Urgently.'

Tahlia's gaze skittered back and forth between Emma and the man behind her. Emma wondered whether she should punish Tahlia and simply not introduce Harry, but it would only cause more questions than it was worth.

'Tahlia Moran, I would like you to meet my old friend, Harry Buchanan.'

Tahlia practically curtsied. 'Harry. Of course. Congratulations on the enormous success of *Harold's House*. It is a supreme example that innovation can still be achieved with the medium. An Internet search engine aimed entirely at under-eighteens. Brilliant!'

Emma couldn't help but grin. Tahlia was such a sweetheart. Such a hard worker. So entrenched in the fabric of WWW Designs. In her capacity as Director of Sales, she was the public face of the company. Emma worried about what would happen if WWW Designs really did come under serious threat. Though she had been one person never to become embroiled in Raquel's 'special assignments', her friend's fall would be so public.

Harry gave Tahlia a brief nod but said no more. Funny. For a guy who usually lapped up female attention as if it was drinking water, the bestowal of praise for his outstanding success seemed to be something he could not simply charm his way through. It was actually kind of adorable.

'Later, T,' Emma said, waving her friend away and stepping into the lift.

'Have fun, Emma,' Chrystal called out, leaning so far over the reception desk Emma could make out the colour of her bra. 'Don't do anything I wouldn't do!'

Emma took Harry by the hand and dragged him into the lift with her. She did all she could to hide her blush. If she followed Chrystal's advice she and her Harry would be in for a wild time.

CHAPTER TWO

*GIRLS' NIGHT IN WITH **THE PRINCESS BRIDE***
'As she wishes? That princess has no idea how lucky she
is,' Keely said. 'The most romantic thing my first
boyfriend said to me was, ''What would you like to watch on
telly?'''

ONCE Emma was finally able to extricate herself from the
WWW Designs building she walked Harry quickly away
from the riverside boardwalk, past the long run of funky
restaurants and hip cafés, and around the corner into the
maze of car parks and parklands behind the office building.

The letter in her briefcase burned in her mind and she
wondered if she should show Harry. But it was a private
letter, one even she should not have seen, so she decided to
let it simmer in her mind for a while longer before involving
anyone else.

'So where are we going in such a hurry?' Harry asked.
'Are you luring me into the bushes for a reason?'

'You wish,' she said, but she slowed only once she knew
they were out of sight of the many beady eyes watching
them through the tenth-storey windows. Spying a park
bench, Emma led Harry to it and sat, dumping her briefcase
on the ground at her feet.

'Now let me have a look at you,' Harry said, taking her
by the hands as he gave her a steady once-over. 'Let's see
how my little princess has aged.'

Emma faced her very best friend, the person who knew

19

her better than any other, and the man who had held her heart in his hand for over a decade. Harry stared right back, his usual unsuspecting smile glinting in his beautiful hazel eyes. She had to look away lest her terrible poker-face disclose how overwhelmed she felt on seeing him again. Instead she focused on the play of light and shadow on the leafy ground as she waited for a mixture of comments about wrinkles, crow's feet and other signs of old age.

But all he said was, 'You are looking spectacular, princess.'

There was an intensity to his voice that had Emma's gaze swinging back to his. But she must have imagined it. He was grinning from ear to ear, his face full of pride, just like the big brother he considered himself to be.

Letting one hand go, he reached out and took a handful of her straight blonde bob. 'Very sophisticated.'

He gave it a little tug before letting the hair slip between his fingers. Emma suppressed a delicious shiver but she could not stop herself from tucking the now swinging hair safely back behind her ear.

'And you haven't changed a bit,' she said. 'I swear you were wearing exactly the same clothes when you drove off a year ago.'

Harry looked down and grinned. Grabbing the flaps of his jacket he opened them up, revealing a fitted white T-shirt clinging to the despicably well-formed chest beneath. 'I think you're probably right.'

'How you get by looking like that I'll never know.'

'I've never had complaints from the ladies before.' He smiled so wide she caught sight of a sexy pair of sharp canines.

'*I* am a lady, so consider this your first. Please let me take you shopping while you're here,' Emma begged.

'Sure,' he said, thankfully covering himself back up. 'Now you are such a sophisticate, maybe you finally can teach me a thing or two.'

'Are you insinuating I never could before?'

He shrugged. 'Well, you are younger than I, and less worldly-wise. What good is it having an older friend unless they can teach you the ways of the world?'

'Please,' she scoffed. 'What did you ever teach me but how to get into trouble?'

'Moi?' he asked, his expression mortified.

'So you want a list? Okay. I can count cards with the best of them thanks to your tutelage the summer I turned fifteen. You taught me how to hotwire a motorbike when I was nineteen. The first time we met you gave me a red apple you had stolen from the next door neighbour's tree.'

'It had fallen into your yard,' he argued.

'The tree was ten feet from our fence! Ruling out a freak hurricane, that was a physical impossibility.'

'Okay then. I am a bad influence. Should I leave now, head hung in shame, never to disgrace your door again?'

Even said in jest the suggestion made Emma's mind mist over red. She reached out and grabbed his hand, tucking it tight between her own. 'Don't even joke about that, Buchanan.'

His smile shifted, lost some of its fashioned charm, and Emma felt the sounds of the park slip away. When he looked at her like that, with such honesty, it gave her ideas. Hope. It made her think that maybe one day he would see her as something other than a little sister type.

He patted her hand. 'You couldn't get rid of me if you tried.' Then he winked and the charmer was back.

The sounds of the park rushed back in. Leaves rustled, birds squawked and cars whooshed past on the road nearby.

'Did you drive over from…wherever you were?' Emma asked, pulling her hands from his as she shifted her weight to the other bottom cheek.

'Yep. I brought the bike. I went by your folks' place on the way here but no one was home.'

'They've gone away.' She could have fitted a golf ball into Harry's rounded mouth.

'Away?' he repeated. 'But they'll be back by Saturday… Surely.'

Saturday. The real reason why Harry came home the same time each year.

Emma shook her head. 'No, they won't. They have taken a much needed break in the Great Barrier Reef for a couple of months.' She watched Harry closely, embroiled in his reaction, which was a great deal fiercer than she would have expected. His brow crinkled, his skin came over blotchy as though he was trying to hold in his acute angst.

'Whose…whose idea was this?'

'Mine. Theirs. I don't remember. We were talking one night about how long it had been since they'd taken a holiday together so I bought them the airfares for their wedding anniversary. They chose this time of year and I didn't once think of asking them to postpone.'

It made sense, it had symmetry and it showed great strength, Emma thought. In choosing not to be in town on that particular Saturday, her parents had made a point that despite past events they were living their lives. She was so proud of them and she wasn't going to let Harry convince her otherwise.

Ready to move on conversationally and physically, Emma gathered her bits and pieces. 'Well, now, dear boy, your forfeited side trip means that you get the surprise early.'

'Surprise?' he asked, taking her briefcase from her.

'A good surprise,' she said, leading the way back to the street where Harry's custom-built motorbike awaited them.

She grabbed the spare helmet and secured the cord under her chin. Harry tied down her briefcase then hopped on and unhooked the kickstand with the ease of an expert. Emma swung her leg over the bike to sit behind him. She wrapped her arms about his waist and she was in her favourite place in the whole world.

Harry covered her arm with one of his own as he turned his head. 'So where to, princess?'

'St Kilda.'

'And what's in St Kilda?'

'My big surprise. I've moved out of home. I have my own apartment and this time around you're staying with me.'

Harry drove five kilometres under the speed limit the whole way. He needed every extra second possible to pull himself together.

Though Emma had ridden behind him on his various motorbikes over the years, this time it felt different. Through her thin suit fabric and his thinning old jacket he could feel her breasts pressed up against him, and having the words 'Emma' and 'breasts' in his head at the one time was not a situation he had been counting on.

It seemed that little Emma was not so little any more. The girl he had always thought of as his kid sister looked like she had grown up overnight. Gone was the cuddly girl with the hair down to her waist and wide blue eyes that looked up to him for guidance about everything from job prospects to her love of drawing to boys, and in her place was this urbane woman with something in her eyes he had never seen before. Was it wisdom? Or maturity? Or experience? He wiped that thought from his mind as quickly as he could.

Considering he hadn't seen her since the same time the year before, he should have seen it coming. She had always been a cute girl, cute enough to whisper at the edge of his awareness repeatedly over the years, but he had long since shouted down those whispers with the memory of why he had no right to be thinking that way about her. So he probably had seen the changes coming and had ignored them outright. But now he could feel Emma's warm body wrapped about him and, as if that was not distraction enough, he was driving her to an apartment. Where she lived alone. Where according to her, he would be sleeping for the next week.

He was surprised at how that news had startled him. She was, what, twenty-four? Of course she had her own place. It was about time. The sweetheart had kept her parents company, looking after their every concern, sorting out problems before they even knew they existed, playing the good girl for longer than anyone could have asked.

Helping those in need was Em's defining quality. She was always looking out for everyone else's interests before her own. He knew, despite her brave face, that having her parents so far away at this time of year had to have been distressing, but so long as they were happy she would never think to disapprove.

She tapped his shoulder as they came up to a red four-storey building a couple of streets away from the beach. He pulled into the driveway and felt a welcome rush of fresh air at his back as she uncurled her soft body from behind him. He grabbed her briefcase and his old leather backpack from the back of his bike and followed her up the steps, his eyes raking over the building and the grounds—anywhere but on her casually swaying hips, which were wrapped in some unbelievable stretch fabric which he was pretty certain was designed less to clothe and more to stun unsuspecting men.

She turned to him at the top of the stairs with the key in the door. 'Ready?' she asked.

Her dazzling grin relaxed him no end. It was young and girlish and reminded him that this was Emma. Little Emma. Sweet Emma. Princess Emma. The girl he had berated when he had caught her smoking at age fifteen. The girl who would do anything he asked, and he had something pretty tricky he was about to ask.

He rubbed his hands together. 'Ready and raring.'

'Now, it's only tiny so don't get too excited. But please feel free to get very excited as, although it's tiny, I love it.'

He crossed his arms and waited for her gushing to cease.

'Sorry,' she said. 'Just come in.' She opened the door with a flourish and welcomed him into her home like the ringmaster in a circus.

The mushroom-coloured walls were so clean he could tell the place had been recently painted, and the dark wood furniture and white couch had that just-purchased look about them. But the thing that caught his attention the second he walked in were the ceiling-to-floor shelves lining one whole wall, surrounding and swamping the small television. The shelves held enough DVDs to fill a rental store.

He stepped up and ran a finger over the spines. *Funny Girl. How to Steal a Million. The Fifth Element.* All romance films. There were comedies, tragedies, action adventures, but they were all romantic. His face warmed with a smile. Trust sweet Em to throw herself into a collection like that.

'So what do you think?' she asked, her brow furrowed in such adorable concern.

'Do you really *own* all of these movies?'

She glared at him, her hands on her hips. 'No. I rented each and every one and never took them back. Of course I own them all. Now, what…do…you…think?'

'It's a very exciting apartment,' he promised.

She gave a little nod. 'That's better.' She threw her keys on the hall table and he followed her down the hallway.

She disappeared inside one room off to the right, singing sweetly under her breath, something familiar and pretty that reminded him of a chick flick she had forced him to sit through once. Harry followed at a distance.

Finally she poked her head out into the hall. 'Come on, slowcoach. The grand tour will only take about thirty seconds, even if you look under every cushion and open every cupboard door.'

He did as he was told and came upon her in what was obviously her bedroom. Gone were the teddy bears and pink lace from her room at her parents' place; instead, her bedroom was all dark wood and coffee-coloured linen. The word that came to mind was *inviting*. He remained resolutely in the hallway.

Emma peeled off her suit jacket and flung it on to her queen-sized bed. She wore a white tailored business shirt that hugged some seriously attractive curves. He had had no idea she had such a tiny waist, which was only accentuated by the not so tiny area above. Harry's gaze lifted so fast it hit the ceiling.

'What are you looking for all the way up there?' she asked.

'Spiders' webs in the corners,' was the best he could come up with.

'Come on, Harry. You know I'm a neat freak.'

But when Harry looked back at her she had her hands on her hips and was glancing about the ceiling, just in case. His mouth lifted in a smile. He could work her so easily. Of course that came from knowing her for over a decade.

He had a sudden flash memory of the first time they had met—he had been coming back to Jamie's place after footy practice one afternoon and had been bowing to one of Jamie's regular dares; this time he'd been ordered to jump the neighbour's fence and return with an apple from their treasured tree.

He had acquiesced instantly, returning with three apples instead. He remembered Jamie's easy grin and absolute appreciation at being beaten. Their strong friendship had been forged in that moment.

Before they had reached the front door it had opened with a slam and a small girl with thick blonde hair to her waist and a mouth full of braces stood on the step, hands on hips, bright blue eyes flashing.

'You're late. Mum is going to kill you!' she had promised, obviously relishing the thought.

Jamie had pushed past, ruffling the girl's hair. 'Squirt, this is Harry. Harry, this is my sister, Emma. She's eleven going on twenty-one,' Jamie had thrown over his shoulder as he disappeared into the kitchen to bury his head in the fridge.

Emma had turned her attention to Harry. 'You don't go to our school,' she had said in a tone so accusing that Harry had had to bite back a laugh.

'No, I don't. I play footy with your brother.'

She had shot a disgusted look over her shoulder at the mention of the boy who was obviously the bane of her existence. 'Poor you,' she had said.

Harry remembered feeling this strange need to impress. She'd been a kid, all metal mouth and attitude, not like the lissom senior girls who were the usual witnesses to his daring and athletic feats, but it didn't stop him throwing the three apples into the air, juggling them, landing two down his footy jersey and one in his mouth. He'd taken a big bite then tossed it to her.

She'd caught the apple in her small hands, looked at it for a moment, looked back at him, took a great big bite herself then disappeared into the house, leaving the door open for him to follow. That was the moment he had first been invited into her house and into her life. Into Jamie's house. Into Jamie's life…

Harry breathed in deep through his nose as he fought his way out of the suddenly stifling memory to find Emma watching him with those same bright blue eyes, only now they were framed by beguiling black lashes highlighted by clever use of mascara.

She looked back at him in silence. The stunning prettiness of her baby blues had never been able to disguise her fierce intelligence, but there was more to her stare now. Standing there before him, all grown up, she now knew exactly what those eyes could do to a guy. He had a sudden flash of something that felt a heck of a lot like attraction.

He spun on his heel and took off. 'So which one's my room? I'm hoping it's decked out with leopard skin walls and shag pile carpet on the ceiling.'

He risked a glance over his shoulder and found Emma watching him with a blank expression. Not quite the indulgent grin he'd been hoping for, but at least it was easier to handle than whatever had been zapping between them moments before.

She pointed across the hall to a room with a single bed,

pink bedspread, yellow floral curtains and a white chest of drawers with *I love Robbie Williams* stickers all over it. So her old room at home had in fact come along for the ride.

'Well, not so much leopard skin as I had hoped.' He jumped as he felt Emma sidle up behind him. He caught a whiff of head-turning perfume but had little time to take pleasure in it as she gave him a slap on the shoulder so hard it would no doubt leave a red mark.

'Haven't quite got to this room in my decorating mania,' she said. She pointed out the room's accoutrements. 'Cupboard. Chest of drawers.' Then she reached around him to point out a small empty box on the bedside table. 'Somewhere to keep your mess of notes.'

It took a moment before he realised what she meant. He reached into his top jacket pocket and pulled out a mishmash of ideas for the evolution of his website that he had jotted down on torn off bits of newspaper and truck stop napkins on the long ride down from Alice Springs.

He put the papers in the tray and his jacket felt a good deal lighter. *Huh. Well, what do ya know?*

'You will stay, won't you?' she asked.

He heard the hint of concern in her voice and he had no choice. He reached to gather his little Emma to him, sighing deeply as she snuggled into him, resting her head against his chest.

'Of course I'll stay, princess. For you, anything.'

Emma released a great breath, the warm air tickling at his skin through his cotton T-shirt. 'I am very glad to hear that.'

But there was more he had to say, and soon, before everything settled and became too chummy. He pulled Emma away and slowly set her down on the edge of the bed. When she looked back at him with such trust he gave in to temptation and ran his hand over the back of her head, revelling in the feel of her soft hair playing against his fingertips.

'Em,' he said, pulling his hand away and distancing himself again, 'keeping in mind my generosity in allowing you to put me up for the week, I have a favour to ask.'

She tilted her head and raised a pale blonde eyebrow. 'Shoot.'

Harry began to pace. *How to ask? How to begin? At the beginning seemed as good a place as any.*

'About six months ago,' he said, 'a *gentleman* sued me, for stealing the idea of *Harold's House* from him.'

Emma felt her stomach drop away and her fighting instincts rose. 'But of course you didn't take the idea from anyone else!' she cried. 'I was there the day *Harold's House* was born. Don't you remember?'

'I remember, sweetheart. But when you have the appearance of power and money you attract the attention of those who seek both. Anyway, it never went to court. He had no case. Nevertheless his stunt brought about enough publicity that I began to receive attention from one woman who believed I was wronged. She began by sending me letters via the *Harold's House* email address.'

Emma reached out and grabbed his hand, stopping him pacing before he left a track in the carpet. She felt him straining against her hold, but she also felt the angry heat welling from inside him. She used her own power to tug him over to sit next to her on the bed.

'The emails became excessive enough they were brought to my attention,' he continued, 'but by that time her attention had already expanded to include handwritten love letters lathered in perfume and gifts of odd souvenirs she had found in small towns as she made her way from Sydney to me. She eventually tracked me down in Alice Springs.'

He glanced over at her and she saw a flash of uncertainty. He was wondering how much to tell her. It must have been pretty bad. 'Tell me, Harry. Please.'

He rolled his shoulders and went somewhere inside himself to draw on experiences obviously buried down deep. 'My core creative group had come out to Alice Springs for a week to get a feel for the place, and thus for the new additions I wanted for the site. We were eating at a local pub one night and she found me sitting at a table with one of my copywriters, Rikki. This woman came straight over, grabbed Rikki by the hair, tore her from her seat and began beating her. It was so unexpected, it took us a few shocked moments before the rest of us dived in to fend her off. By that stage she had already split Rikki's lip and broken a rib.'

'Oh, my God! Harry!' Emma felt a sense of cold dread gripping her spine that the woman might still be out there somewhere, thinking of Harry, watching Harry, planning to hurt Harry. Her fists clenched in her lap as she thought what she would do to the woman if she ever got her hands on her. 'Where is this woman now?'

'The police arrested her in Alice Springs. It turned out she was a serial stalker. She had pulled a similar stunt with some football jock in New South Wales and was wanted for kidnapping the guy's girlfriend. Now she is behind bars and those around me are safe from her attention.'

He squeezed her hand and she knew he was making sure she realised she was safe. Emma felt a heady sense of relief. 'And Rikki?'

'She's fine. All better. She's even still working for me, believe it or not.'

There was one more thing she had to know. 'Was she…are you and Rikki…together?'

He shook his head and her relief doubled. 'Never. But it didn't matter. This woman was so obsessed it didn't matter.'

'Harry, how can I not know this sort of stuff? You are supposed to be my best friend and yet you haven't let me help you through any of the tough stuff.'

'What good can it do burdening you, Em? I would rather that sweet mind of yours was filled with nice thoughts. Ignorance is bliss.'

'Please!' Emma scoffed. 'I would much rather be in the know, to be able to help you and know you than to be in the dark.'

Harry's smile was full of sadness. 'But that's just it, Em. I don't bring good luck to those who care for me.'

'That woman didn't care for you!'

'No, she didn't. But others have.'

Emma knew exactly who he meant. Jamie. But that was ridiculous. He couldn't possibly still be so defined by that experience, could he?

'That's half the reason I couldn't come to your surprise party, Em. Keely had tracked me down and invited me. But when all this happened, I had to pull out. There was nothing that would have brought me back to you with that sort of danger following close behind.'

She believed him. He hadn't come to her party in order to protect her. How ironic. It was one of the many times he had broken her heart in the name of trying to look out for her best interests.

'So now for my favour,' he said. 'You must know I have been nominated for this competition, this Australia's Best Bachelor thing.'

Emma grinned. Trust him to not even know the name of the biggest, most highly publicised event in the country.

Harry caught her grin. 'Hey,' he said, 'I have been told

on the odd occasion that I can be quite hunky when the light is right.'

Emma smiled. Harry didn't need anything as transitory as light, nor something as subjective as a competition to make him look hunky. He made Emma's heart race just by looking her in the eye.

'Oh, it's not that, Buchanan. I'm sure that under the right circumstances you can come across downright hunky to someone with the sun in their eyes. It's just that WWW is heavily involved with that comp.'

'I know, Em, and that's why I am hoping that you can do something to get me out of it.'

Emma opened her mouth but no words came out. She hadn't seen that one coming at all. 'Are you serious?'

'Dead serious, Em,' he said. 'I haven't done an interview since this whole business played itself out, and I don't want to start now. Especially in a forum where I am to be held up as an object of…interest to women. *Harold's House* will happily thrive without any focus on me, so if there is anything you can do to get me out of this thing, cleanly and quickly, I would appreciate it.'

It seemed that Emma now had not only the future of WWW Designs weighing on her, but she was being called upon to jeopardise WWW's involvement with *Flirt* magazine, the account for which nothing could go wrong. *But what else could she do?*

'Of course I'll help, Harry,' Emma said, repeating his promise of moments before. 'For you, anything.'

CHAPTER THREE

TAHLIA'S SUNDAY NIGHT RITUAL:
MR DARCY AND A DAIQUIRI
'It is a truth universally acknowledged that a single man
in possession of a good fortune must *be in want of a wife? I*
dare Jane Austen to come over here and say that to my face,'
Tahlia said as she slammed Pride and Prejudice *shut and hid*
it under her sofa cushion.. this time for a full ten seconds.

EMMA left Harry to unpack.

Once she heard the shower running, she changed out of her suit and into cut-off jeans. She sat on the edge of her bed, still topless apart from her bra, staring at some point on her wall as the synapses in her brain buzzed and flickered, trying to assimilate the spate of news that had come her way in the past couple of hours, and trying to conceive of some way to fix all situations for the best.

Harry wanted nothing to do with the Australia's Hunkiest Bloke competition and for good reason. So how could she help get him out of it? The rules of the competition were pretty easygoing. The editors chose the nominees and the readers chose the winner. The guys in question didn't have to do anything but exist. They didn't even have to turn up to the big announcement party on Saturday night, though most of them had already RSVPd. To get her Harry out of the running would be tricky. The only prerequisites were that the guys had to be Australian, hunky and single, and Harry fit into every category perfectly.

Her mobile phone chirped in her handbag. The ring tone, *Copacabana*, in her opinion the most romantic song ever written, beeped merrily away until she answered it. 'Aloha?'

'Aloha yourself,' Keely said from the other end.

'Are we disturbing you?' Tahlia asked, hope lacing her voice. It seemed this was a check-up conference call.

'Please. What do you think?' Emma said, slumping back on to her big beautiful unchristened bed. 'He's taking a shower and—'

'Well, now's your big chance,' Keely insisted, her voice rising with excitement. 'Go in there. Join him. Naked and wet there will be nowhere for him to run!'

Tahlia joined Emma in her silent stupor.

'You have to be kidding me,' Emma finally managed.

'Well, you are only madly in love with him. Joining him for a soap and scrub will put him in no doubt.'

'That's for sure. Just as surely it will scare him back to the other side of the country before the sun sets.'

'Fine,' Keely acquiesced. 'But just know that we are here for you with advice, hugs, chocolate and constant reminders that you ought to go for it. It will be the best thing you ever did for yourself. Take my word for it.'

Emma's synapses were making progress. Brainstorming with the girls always helped and, just like that, the way to help Harry opened up before her. It wouldn't be the easiest path, thus she needed moral support. 'Guys, I have something important to run by you. We have to find a way out of the *Flirt* competition for Harry.' Emma went on to explain why.

Keely sucked in a sharp breath. 'Jeez, Em! I had no idea. That's why he had the sudden turn-around about coming to your party. The poor guy was keeping you from the clutches of a crazy stalker. How sweet!'

'Anyway,' Emma said, 'I think I have found a way out, but I'm going to need your help.'

'Why do I have a bad feeling about this?' Tahlia asked.

'Because you don't want to do anything to jeopardise your precious promotion chances,' Keely blurted. 'Come on, T. Sometimes it's good to be bad. I'm in, Em. What do you want us to do?'

Emma took a deep breath and blurted out her idea. 'I am going to suggest to Harry that we become engaged.'

The silence on the other end of the phone was deafening, from both sources. Emma leapt in to fill the silence. 'Temporarily,' she added. 'Just to make him ineligible. Can I rely on you guys to tell anyone who asks that we have had a long distance relationship for the last few months and are madly in love and you saw this coming from a mile away? Guys?'

'What do you get out of this?' Tahlia finally asked.

'The opportunity to help a friend in need,' Emma said.

'A friend for whom you would lay down in traffic if that was what he wanted,' Keely reminded her. 'Em, are you sure you aren't just setting yourself up for heartache here?'

'Hey, this was my idea, guys. Not his. I'm not even sure if he will go for it, but I don't see any other way out and he's been through enough already. So can I count on you to support me?'

'Of course, sweetheart,' Tahlia finally acquiesced. 'So long as you also know that we'll be there to scrape you off the road and supply you with sickening amounts of conciliating chocolate after this whole charade ends and Harry has gone back into hiding.'

Emma heard a funny crackle down the phone line. 'What's that noise?'

Keely piped up. 'Um, it's some of that chocolate we were talking about. I felt the sudden need to taste test.'

Emma heard a familiar snap.

'It's really good,' Keely promised with a mouthful.

'Aren't you guys meant to be working?' Emma asked.

'Aren't you?' Keely shot back.

'Okay. Point taken.'

The shower stopped.

'I'd better go. See you guys tomorrow morning.'

'Breakfast at Sammy's?' Tahlia asked.

'Sure. Usual time.'

'Be strong!' Keely called out.

'Thanks, guys. Bye.' Emma hung up.

There was a light knock at Emma's door. Emma jumped and pulled a white T-shirt over her head. 'Yeah?'

Harry opened the door and popped his head in. He was naked bar a towel wrapped around his waist. 'How about a walk on the beach?' he suggested. 'I've been too far from the coast for too long. I think half the dust from the Northern Territory has just disappeared down your shower drain.'

Emma had no idea what words had come out of his mouth. Her brain was pretty much filled with an expanse of male chest. Why on earth had she asked him to stay with her? She knew he did stuff like this. Even at her folks' place. The guy was shameless. Did she really think she could manage to spend one week under the same roof with the guy, alone, and not completely collapse into a nervous wreck?

Yes. She did. She had to. The time had come in her life that she had to do something about this crush of hers once and for all. Keely and Tahlia were on the money. This time she would either tell him how she felt, how she had felt for a number of years, or she would make herself finally get over him. She just wasn't sure yet which way she would go. But if he agreed to her idea, she would go a fair way to finding out.

'Okay,' she said. 'Get dressed and we'll head off.'

Harry closed her door with a soft click and Emma finally collapsed under the weight of her own foolishness and slumped, face down and spread-eagled, on to the bed.

When most families were making their way home from work and school, Emma and Harry walked along the path that snaked around St Kilda beach.

Harry had ditched his jacket and jeans for a long-sleeved T-shirt and knee-length shorts. His flip-flops were spattered with the red dirt of the heart of Australia.

Emma picked up a shell from the pathway and played with it as she walked. 'So you've been in Alice Springs all this time?'

'Most recently.'

'And where before that?'

'Around.'

'Always around. Anywhere more specific? Some town with a name, perhaps?'

Harry shrugged, kicking at a stray tuft of grass growing between a crack in the concrete. 'Kakadu.'

'Seriously? I should have known. The new colour scheme for *Harold's House* is straight out of that part of the country.'

The heavy burnt umbers and rich forest greens of Kakadu National Park, located in the far north of Australia, held a mystical quality which Emma thought Harry's web designers had translated beautifully.

'You go on to the *Harold's House* site much?' he asked. He stepped sideways and gave her a little bump with his hip.

Emma threw the shell back on to the sand and wiped the sand from her fingers. 'What do you reckon?' Emma asked, bumping him right back. 'Of course I do. It's my home page.'

Harry poked out his bottom lip and nodded. 'Cool.'

Emma could see it was more than cool. The guy was thrilled. He really had no idea how much of an impact he had on her. 'Is there much of a market for computer whiz-kids in the Kakadu?'

'Unfortunately, it seems there is. I was there a week before a local paper found out and by the next day I was inundated with requests for help, with job offers, with promotional opportunities and...other things.'

Unwelcome new acquaintances, Emma thought.

'I almost said yes to becoming the spokesman for an exciting new real estate opportunity out there.'

'Seriously?'

Harry stopped walking. 'Of course not! And if you ask me if I'm serious one more time I'm going to throw you over my shoulder and see if that water is as cold as it looks.'

Emma stared back, the desire to test his threat tickling at her throat. Harry's eyes narrowed and he shifted his stance as though ready to attack her at a moment's notice. It was enough for her to back down. She knew from long experience that he didn't make idle threats.

'Okay,' she said, ambling away once more, 'I'm sorry. I'm just as interested as the next guy about what Wonder Boy Buchanan will come up with next.'

'Don't hold your breath,' he said, though so quietly she might have been mistaken. '*Harold's House* is plenty for me to concentrate on. I now have an agent, a business manager and a mishmash of forty-odd staff scattered throughout Victoria. The site is growing exponentially by the day. It's a monster. It's bigger than I ever envisioned.' He shook his head back and forth and Emma knew he had no idea how he had become such a success.

But she knew. All his ventures, all of his crazy stunts, all of his mad, slapdash efforts to forge out a career for himself, had thrived. But this one had gone stratospheric, because it came straight from his heart. The site's cheeky language, glorious Australian backdrops and ever-evolving layout were all so much a part of the sun-drenched Aussie man that he was.

'Seriously?' Emma asked, skewing the mood back towards fun.

Harry's discomposure was gone in a heartbeat. He turned to her with a toothy grin. 'That's it, kiddo. You've done it now.'

Emma squealed and leapt on to the sand and took off down the beach at full pelt. Harry caught up with her in no time. He grabbed her around the waist and all her twisting was to no avail. With a quick heave and an overdone grunt, Harry had her over his shoulder. She kicked out, trying her best to get away.

'Harry, put me down or I will kick you where it'll hurt you most.'

'Nup. You had fair warning, princess. You are going for a swim.'

They had reached the edge of the surf; Emma could see it tickling at Harry's feet. 'Come on, Harry. I am giving you food and shelter for the week. Is this how you are going to repay me?'

He hovered and she knew she had him.

'Put me down, Harry, and I will never question your seriousness again.'

'Fine,' he said, groaning loudly as he slid her to the ground. 'I'm going to hold you to that, little one.'

Emma landed on the soft sand to find herself bodily up against him. One hand rested on his shoulder the other around his neck. His hands remained casually around her waist. An ocean breeze played with his hair.

A wondering smile lit Harry's eyes as he looked down upon her. 'Though you really aren't my little one any more, are you?'

Emma's heart beat so raggedly in her chest she was certain Harry must have felt it too. He leant away and her hands naturally slipped down on to his chest. If they were any other couple in the world it would have been the most perfect moment for a kiss.

Then he glared at her through slitted eyes. 'You're bloody heavy, Emma! At the very least you're a stone heavier than the last time I had you in a fireman's lift.' He moved out of her grasp and bent from the waist with his hands massaging his lower back.

It hit Emma with the force of a thunderclap that they weren't any other couple. They were Harry and Em, the terrible two, a couple of mates who knew each other so well they could finish off one another's sentences. It would take more than a haircut, a new apartment and an ocean breeze to make Harry see differently.

She sucked up her disappointment and did her best to look as if she was sharing the same joke. 'I was fourteen years old the last time you had me over your shoulder.'

'Hmm,' he said, straightening up, a flirtatious grin knocking the breath from her lungs. 'It's obviously been too long between times. I'll have to rectify that in the future.'

Emma felt as if she was on the pirate ship ride at the fairground—one minute Harry's little one, the next on the receiving end of one of his killer smiles. He reached out and gave her a jab in the side. He was a natural flirt, she reminded herself. She was just in the line of fire. She flinched away. 'Stop it!'

'Just checking where all that extra weight is distributed.'

'It's distributed exactly where it should be,' she shot back, sticking out her chest to prove it.

If she was any other girl his gaze would have warmed before travelling over all the bits of her that should have grown since puberty. But he merely gave her a brief smile before looking decidedly at the bridge of her nose.

Unable to cope with the rising innuendos, Emma grabbed him by the arm and led him over to a patch of flat rocks at the top of the sand. 'Come on, boyo, I think you need to sit for a bit. All this exercise is making you say things you don't mean.'

Though the sun was warm, the ground was chilly, which was fine with Emma. She dug her feet into the fine beige sand and let it cool her from the toes up. They sat in companionable silence for a few minutes, watching the sun set over the flat waters of Port Philip Bay.

'This is new,' Harry finally said, reaching and giving the second toe on her right foot a wiggle.

Emma glanced at her gold toe ring. 'Mmm. It was a birthday present. Do you like it?' she asked, waving it so close to his nose he had to bat it away.

'You look like a homing pigeon,' he finally said, grabbing her by the ankle and dragging her foot on top of his thighs where he gave it a casual massage.

The tingles running unabated through Emma were anything but casual. Feigning the need to stretch, she moved her foot away from his warm hands until it rested innocently next to her other.

'Who was it from?' he asked.

'A friend.'

'What sort of friend?' The look Harry shot her was hooded, dark, jealous? Emma's heart thumped against her ribs.

'It was a pressie from Tahlia.'

'Which one was she again?' he asked, his eyes lighting with mischief. 'The single one?'

'Yes,' Emma agreed through clenched teeth. 'But don't get any ideas. I share no secrets from Keely and Tahlia. So they know way too much about you for your comfort.'

He gave an exaggerated shiver and silence reigned once more.

'So have you thought any more—?' Harry said.

'Speaking of Keely and Tahlia—' Emma said at the same time.

They stopped, and laughed.

'Ladies first,' Harry insisted.

Emma turned so that one leg was tucked beneath her. 'Okay. I think I have come up with a solution for your problem, but I'm not sure you're going to like it as it's kind of bizarre. Ready?'

'Ready and raring,' Harry insisted, his eyes crinkling down at her so beautifully she found it hard to bring herself to say the words.

Somewhere in the back of her mind, becoming engaged to Harry had been her dream. Since she was a little girl, playing with her Ken and Barbie dolls, listening to her Mum's Barry Manilow records, she had always dreamed that one day this moment would come. But not quite like this. Never quite like this. She wondered if in proposing this charade to Harry she wasn't once and for all giving up on her dream. But what could she do? Harry was in dire straits and it seemed she was the only one who could help him. She had no choice.

'So what can we do to get me out of this thing?' Harry asked.

'Harry, you have to get yourself a fiancée.'

She waited for him to laugh, or blanch, or run for his life, but he merely watched her, closely, carefully, as he let the idea sink in. Then, after only a few moments, he began to nod.

'If I am engaged, I am no longer eligible. Ha! You are brilliant!' He reached out, grabbed her by the shoulders and planted a great smacking kiss on her cheek, but when he pulled away she saw the uncertainty in his eyes.

'But who could I become engaged to at such short notice? Someone who wouldn't get any ideas. Someone who could make it believable. At least until the whole shebang is over. At least until Saturday.'

His gaze skittered out into the distance, his hazel eyes lit gold by the sun shining off the ocean. Emma waited patiently for him to make the final leap to the other half of her plan. The scary half.

He still had a hold of her shoulders and finally his gaze swung back to land upon her. She watched as the idea came full circle. His Adam's apple bounced in his throat and his gaze hungrily devoured her face, as though realising she was really there, sitting so close to him.

'Em. Princess. I hate to ask, but do you think…?'

She couldn't bear to see him struggling so. 'Of course, you great lump, it's the only thing that makes sense. Keely and Tahlia are prepared to go along with any story we concoct so it should be a breeze.'

'So, you and me, hey?'

Emma nodded. 'Until Saturday night, we will be affianced. If you are okay with it.'

Then Harry smiled. One of those radiant, happy ever after, lit from within smiles that turned her bones to butter and returned time and again in her daydreams. He pulled her to him and hugged her tight. 'Thanks, Em. You have saved me. If there is anything I can ever do to return the favour...'

Enjoying the feel of his warmth wrapping itself about her like a blanket on an autumn night, Emma was loath to pull away. But there was more she had to say, more that she had not shared with her best friends, more that with Harry's help they would never need to know.

With great effort she extricated herself from his heavenly embrace. 'Well, now that you mention it...'

Harry's smile shifted from radiant delight to insightful good spirits. 'Okay. Here it goes. What's your fee, princess? Money? Jewels? Foot rubs every day for a year?'

The foot rub idea almost won out! But Emma had to take Harry's offer while it was on the table.

'Nothing like that, Buchanan. It is something infinitely more delicate, and more important to me.'

Picking up on her tone, Harry's business face slipped into place and she had his rapt attention at once.

'I had a really odd conversation with my boss this morning,' Emma began, 'and I think that WWW Designs might be in trouble.'

'Did she say as much?'

'Not really, but Raquel is usually rather...abrupt and this morning she was almost giving me a kindly warning. It freaked me out more than her yelling ever would. Then I found some concrete evidence in the form of a legal letter.

Raquel has brought some heavy problems down upon the business.'

'Have you talked to the girls about it?'

Emma's hand flew to her chest. 'No. I wouldn't want to worry them.'

Harry nodded. 'Of course, *you* wouldn't want to worry anybody.' Then, 'So what can I do to help?'

'I was thinking, the only way out, the only thing I could do to help, the only extra big, huge difference I could make at such short notice to bring WWW Designs a boost, would be to bring on board the biggest thing in web design right now.'

Harry stopped nodding. He knew exactly who she meant. It was all he ever heard. He wasn't just Harry Buchanan any more. He was Harry Buchanan, wunderkind creator of *Harold's House*. But he didn't say so. Emma leapt into the silence before he had the chance.

'I was thinking that WWW could help run *Harold's House* for you. You said it had become too big for your small team to handle. I've been thinking about it all afternoon. The whole top floor of our lease is empty right now. We could clean it out. Do it up. You would have the privacy of rooms to yourselves with the backing of a superb team of designers behind you. So why don't you guys come on over to us? It's win win.'

'I'll do it,' he said instantly.

'Really?' Emma squealed, grabbing him by the upper arms.

'Sure,' he said with a shrug. 'Why not? We've never had a proper base before, with everyone working from all over the place. Southbank is as good a place as any. Close to food, close to the city, close to the football stadium at the Docklands.' *Besides which,* he thought, *the thing is under such momentum I don't think it would matter where we were based.*

Emma suddenly threw herself bodily against him. He was rocked back by the force. His arms came about her naturally, as they had a million times before, but again it felt different. Her hair smelled like peaches and the smooth skin of her face felt too damn nice against his stubble-roughened cheek. So he pulled away.

His reasons for not wanting to be nominated were complicated, more complicated than simply not wanting to attract unwanted attention. He'd had enough of the dog and pony show his fame had created as he knew he didn't deserve a lick of the success that had fallen his way. He would do whatever it took to keep a low profile.

'Okay,' he said. 'Let's shake hands on the deal. Be my fiancée and I will bring my business to WWW Designs. That seems a fair exchange of labour to me, and timely that we both need each other right now. Written in the stars, I'd say.'

I've always thought so, Emma thought. 'Sure,' she said, 'Of course. No worries.'

No worries? Who was she kidding? She had just agreed to be Harry's pretend fiancée. In order to pull the wool over her boss's eyes. Her boss who could make it very hard for her, Tahlia and Keely if she so chose.

She felt like one of those circus performers who spin plates atop a bunch of pointy sticks. She had to keep her plates spinning just right or else the whole lot could crash to the ground and she would be left with nothing but broken crockery.

So far the spinning plates were spinning in the right direction. Bringing *Harold's House* on board would surely help save WWW Designs. It was all good. Everything was fine. Everybody would come out okay in the end.

A couple came into her line of sight. Emma could not help but turn to see where Harry was looking, and was not surprised to find him watching the curvy brunette female half of the couple with an appreciative smile on his face. If that wasn't enough, he let out a smooth whistle, only loud enough for Emma to hear.

She was irked to see he was acting his usual self; he was not in the least affected by their recent conversation. She turned back to the front and concentrated on the man at the brunette's side. He was all dark good looks and bulging muscles. He was empirically hot, but not to her taste at all.

'I agree,' Emma said, keeping her gaze fixed straight ahead. 'That is one gorgeous hunk of man flesh.'

The comment had done its job. Harry's attention shot to her.

'So you like a bit of muscle on your men, do you, little one?'

'You bet.'

Harry went quiet and Emma bit back a triumphant grin.

They watched in silence as the girl, with her upturned nose high in the air, stalked ahead of her beau with as much dignity as one could muster whilst walking through soft dry sand. The man was gesticulating madly, obviously apologising for something that had upset his lady.

Emma sighed as the quarrelling lovers passed from view. 'They are just as I imagine Lola and Tony must have looked.'

Harry deigned to drag his gaze away from the haughty retreating figure. 'Who on earth are Lola and Tony?'

'From *Copacabana*.'

'The Barry Manilow song that you used to play over and over on your Walkman as a kid?'

'The very one. They had such a passionate relationship he was shot defending her.' Emma sighed again and lay back against the flat rocks and stared at the darkening sky. 'It's just too, too romantic.'

'I don't think getting shot and killed is terribly romantic.'

'Dying for the one you love is about as romantic as it gets.'

Harry lay down beside her, propping himself up on his elbow as he looked down at her. 'As far as I remember that song, she spent the rest of her life boozing it up and living in the past.'

'I know. Beautiful, isn't it?' If only Harry knew that was what she was doing for him—laying her breaking heart on the line to help him out of a fix. 'That's what one does for the man one loves.'

'I think it's pretty stupid, actually.'

Emma glared at him from one squinted eye. If only he didn't look so unbearably handsome, with the last of the afternoon sun warming his smiling face, she might very well have reneged on the whole deal then and there. Ungrateful sod! 'You would,' she said.

'What is that supposed to mean?'

'Harry, you don't have one romantic bone in your body.'

He puffed out his chest. 'I would have you know that a high percentage of the women I have dated would consider me highly romantic.'

Emma scoffed. 'The fact that you would bring up the high percentage of women you have dated in front of another woman shows how clueless you are.'

'But you're not *another woman*,' Harry said, his eyes a mixture of hurt innocence.

Charming, she thought as he reiterated exactly what she feared he thought about her. 'You're right,' she said. 'I am your *fiancée*. What was I thinking, Harry? Nobody in their right mind is going to believe you and I are engaged. This whole thing is going to fall in a big heap as soon as *you* have to tell another soul.'

'Em, don't say that.'

She opened her eyes and squinted up at him. He was watching the couple walk away but not with the same wolf-ish expression. Something deep and dark was going on be-hind his gorgeous hazel eyes.

'I'm only telling it like it is, Harry. Maybe we should find another way to get out of our respective situations before we make them sticky rather than just tricky.'

Harry shot to his feet. 'Nope. It will work and I am going to prove it to you.'

That got Emma's attention. She dragged herself up into a sitting position. 'How?'

'Be ready by seven tonight.'

'Ready for what?'

'Just wear something dressy and prepare to be proven wrong.'

With that he was gone. Ten feet in the wrong direction before he realised then turned and headed back towards her apartment.

Emma was a tad concerned about what he had in mind, but only a tad. The rest of her was intrigued and more than a little excited at the thought of her Harry going out of his way to prove to her how romantic he could be.

One second he was buddy-buddy, the next she caught him

watching her with such awareness in his gaze. Which was the real Harry?

She was so confused.

He was so confused.

Harry walked back to Emma's apartment block with his hands deep in his shorts pockets and his head aching from too much brow furrowing.

What on earth was he doing, setting about proving to his little Emma what sort of fiancé he would make? The words had shot from him in a he-man display, the likes of which he had not encountered since his late teens. Odd. Very odd. He had been back for a couple of hours and already he felt as if the whole visit was turning out to be odd.

Sure his life had changed since the last time he had seen Emma, just under a year before. He had been sued, stalked and achieved business success beyond his wildest dreams. But if his life had changed, Emma was a revelation. Then again, maybe she wasn't. She was still the same spitfire, the same girl he had adored and protected as if she was his own sister for going on thirteen years.

He stopped walking. Thirteen years. More than half her life. Had it been that long since he had taken on the big brother role that he still prided himself on today?

He turned and saw Emma strolling behind him about a block away. She held up a hand and gave him a flirty little finger wave. Or maybe it wasn't flirty. Maybe it was just sarcastic, which would be understandable as he *was* acting odd.

He shook out his tightening shoulders. 'Come on, buddy,' he said aloud. 'Relax. Saturday is looming and you have to be strong for her, to make the next week as easy for her as possible. Don't go creating more difficulties for her than you already have. Help save her job. Give her a good time, and if that means taking her out for a night on the town, Harry-style, so be it. That's the least you can do.'

Even though he knew people were looking at him sideways for talking to himself, he headed back to the apartment feeling a little less odd.

CHAPTER FOUR

AFTER SOLO LATE-NIGHT CARY GRANT MARATHON
After having left yet another short-term boyfriend, with
her phone in one hand, Harry's number in the other, and
An Affair to Remember *replaying in her mind, Emma*
wished it was that easy to say hello.

AT SEVEN o'clock Emma sat waiting on the couch. She had washed and blow-dried her hair. She wore a chocolate-brown long-sleeved knee-length dress with a deep V-neck that fitted her like a second skin. She wore a thick rope of tiny aqua beads around her neck, the colour of which she knew made her eyes pop. Her chocolate-coloured stilettos rubbed against her heels as her legs jiggled at an insane rate.

'Ready?'

Emma turned to find Harry standing at the end of the hallway. He wore clean jeans, a clean black T-shirt and his usual caramel leather jacket. He had showered and shaved, the clear skin on his cheeks making him look five years younger and so adorable her sensitive heart twisted tighter still. Track marks of his lazy fingers sliced through his damp hair. The tracks teased, cruelly showcasing exactly where her fingers ached to trawl.

She stood on shaky legs to join him. He leaned in to give her a chummy kiss on the cheek. He smelt of soap and his cheek felt smooth and warm against hers.

Though she was perfectly happy with how he looked in his jeans, she felt ridiculously overdressed. What if he

53

thought *she* thought this was meant to be a real date, not just the evolution of one of his dares? She knew it wasn't, of course, but she had no idea what was running through his mind as his gaze slowly traversed the length and breadth of her body.

'I thought you were meant to be romancing me?' she said, hands on hips, attitude switched to full power to cover her chagrin.

'Give me a chance!' he said.

She held her hands out in submission. 'Okay. Sorry. Go ahead.'

She clasped her hands behind her back and made a big play of waiting patiently. Harry took a deep breath, rolled his shoulder then cast such a sultry glance her way that her cool demeanour was all but undone.

'I was about to tell you how incredibly beautiful you look tonight,' he said, his voice a purr. She would have considered it a throwaway line but for the slightly pink flush that crept up his neck as he looked her over again.

'Were you now?' she said, her voice managing to come out almost normal.

His mouth quirked into a lopsided grin. 'I was until you opened your big trap and ruined the moment.'

'There was a moment? I hadn't noticed.'

His eyes narrowed. 'You are not going to make this easy for me, are you? No worries. I'm all for a challenge.' He held out an elbow, bowing ever so slightly at the waist. Even in his bad boy get-up, charm came to him as easily as breathing. 'Shall we?'

Wondering what on earth she had agreed to, Emma hooked her hand through his elbow, revelling in the texture and scent of the familiar leather. 'It seems that we shall.'

*   *   *

Harry led Emma to a local club he had frequented a couple of years before. He was pretty sure he knew where it was, but with her walking beside him, smelling so good, her hip brushing against his with every second step, he could barely remember what city he was in.

All dolled up she did indeed look beautiful. So beautiful, in fact, that it concerned him. If she dressed like this on her regular nights on the town, she was in danger of...what? Being attractive to any number of men?

The thought made Harry's stomach churn. It was just the big brother nature coming into play. That was all. He had been her protector for so long, this was just another facet to the job—this heated, animalistic, ravenous desire to tear the throat from any man who dared glance her way as she sashayed along the paved footpath.

When the familiar façade of the club came into sight he sighed with relief. Emma looked to him with a questioning expression and he grinned back. When in doubt, grin. The ladies seemed to respond to his wolfish smile, but using it on Emma felt...odd. His grin wavered and fell away. *Come on, buddy. Keep it together.*

'This is the place?' she asked when he hesitated at the front steps.

Suddenly he wondered if this local joint would suffice. After months spent in a town in the Northern Territory where a pub that stocked cold beer was considered plush, this place had seemed a good choice. But this was the shiny new Emma he was dealing with. Oh, well, he hadn't booked a table anywhere else and as it was an unusually balmy night he wouldn't have any luck at such late notice.

'This is the place,' he said. He dislodged her hand from its sincerely comfortable spot in the crook of his arm and with one hand at her back escorted her inside.

The bouncer at the door looked up at their footsteps. 'Hey, Emma! Welcome back.'

Okay. So she knew the place. Fine. A little hiccup on the way to wowing her with romance, but no big deal.

'Hey, Mikey,' she said, giving the large guy a kiss on the cheek. 'I'd like to introduce you to my best mate, Harry. He's staying in town for a week.'

'Great. Well, in you go. Have fun, Harry.'

Harry shot the huge guy a quick salute before following Emma inside. The place was filled to the rafters. Loud eighties music blared from a zillion speakers. Emma reached behind and took Harry's hand as she led him through the throng.

'Come on,' she yelled. 'There's a small bar in the back which is pretty secluded.'

Harry followed as she bopped and boogied her way across the dance floor, stopping every now and then to say *hi* to this person or kiss the cheek of that person. But at least on the pit stops he had a hiatus from watching her hips swaying jauntily to her favourite type of music.

Finally they made it to the bar in the back. Emma made a beeline for an empty tall table and lifted herself atop a high chair. Though dark and atmospheric, it had room to move. The music from the next room thumped through the thin walls but he could talk over the top without having to shout himself hoarse.

Harry grabbed his tattered old wallet. He flicked his wrist in a drinking motion and mouthed, 'Drink?'

She nodded. 'Surprise me.'

'Stay,' he said, pointing to her and squinting his eyes to make sure she knew he was deadly serious. Emma sat on her hands, pursed her lips and nodded like a good girl.

Harry took his time at the bar to collect himself.

Somehow he had ended up on a date with his best friend's little sister. Not a real date, of course, though Emma looked so fine he was hard pressed not to think of it that way. No, it was just a pretend date to prove how romantic he could be, how he could be a believable fiancé so that she would agree to help him out of his fix. Ha! He had set up real dates with other women on a lot less of a premise than that.

Come on, this is Emma, he told himself. *You are here to give her a pep talk. You are her cheerleader, a strong pair of shoulders, nothing more. Give her whatever she needs to have a good time, to feel good about herself, to feel secure in your friendship, to know she can count on you, and then off you go again, to the far side of the world, before you find the whole deal too good to give up.*

'What can I get you, mate?' the young bartender asked.

'Um, a bag of pretzels and…' Harry remembered the delight in Emma's voice when she had said, *'Harry, you don't have one romantic bone in your body.'* She had set the challenge, so it was only fair he do his best to shoot it down in flames. 'A bottle of champers and two glasses— the classiest ones you've got.'

The bartender looked over his shoulder and grinned. Harry followed his gaze to find Emma reading a beer coaster, her legs swinging under her high chair.

'You here with Em?' the guy asked with a smile in his voice.

It was enough for Harry to turn slowly back. 'That I am. Do you know her well?'

The guy shrugged. 'Not as well as I would like.' Then he seemed to realise to whom he was talking. The poor kid's face blushed crimson. 'I just mean she's, you know, one of the good ones.' He cleared his throat. 'A bottle of bubbly, was it?'

'And *two* glasses,' Harry repeated, suppressing the throat-tearing urge once more.

Emma looked up when Harry sat at the table with his yield. 'Ooh,' she gushed. 'Pretzels. Classy! *And* a whole bottle of champagne? Are you planning on getting me drunk?'

'Yep.'

That shut her up. Her whole body sizzled as though her bloodstream was filled with bubbles already. 'Yep?' she repeated. 'Well, I don't know about you, but that's just about the most romantic line *I've* ever heard.'

Harry smiled but he kept his gaze on the glasses he was filling. He passed her a glass of amber bubbles. He held out his own and she felt a toast coming on.

'To Terry and Leanne,' he said.

It took Emma a moment to fathom what he was going on about. 'I hope you mean Tony and Lola of *Copacabana* fame, or I am totally lost.'

'Tony and Lola, eh?' He gave a little shrug, his glittering eyes showing he knew exactly who they were. 'They'll do.'

She clinked his glass and took a large gulp. The bubbles tickled at her throat and only added to the thrill of sitting across the table from the most gorgeous guy she had ever known. But Emma found herself half dreading and half anticipating what he would do next. After all, this was his show.

'So how is work?' he asked out of the blue, bringing her back down to earth.

'Apart from the fact that it might all slip away before we know it?'

'Yeah. Apart from that.'

She took another sip as she thought about the incredible

opportunities she had been given in being able to create characters like Blondie. 'Really very good, actually.'

'So, do you have plans on kicking the pit bull off her perch?'

'The Rottweiler.'

'Okay. The canine in three-inch heels, whichever breed she may be.'

'I'm more than happy doing what I am doing.'

'Hence the desire to keep the place afloat no matter what it takes.'

'Mmm. Though Keely will take some maternity leave when the bub is born, Tahlia is in line for a huge promotion. It's so close we can all taste it for her. I have to do all I can to make sure they are looked after.'

Emma happily tapped her toes in time with the music but she and Harry had settled into the same unusual loaded silence that seemed to be sneaking up on them more and more. Emma sought for something to ask back. 'I know work is going swimmingly for you, but how's your love life?' popped out of her mouth before she could stop herself.

The look he shot her was penetrating and she had to take a pretty large gulp of champagne in order to disconnect from it.

'Quiet,' he said, his voice laced with concern, and Emma only then remembered the harrowing experience he had recently endured with his stalker.

'Apart from the fact that I am engaged to you?' she reminded him, attempting to draw him back to the present.

'Oh, yeah,' he said, a smile illuminating his downcast eyes. 'Quiet, apart from that.'

Emma shook her head. 'If I can't even get *you* to remember we are engaged, how will anyone else believe it? I know. You can dance with me!'

'Nup. Don't dance.'

Emma bounced up and down on her chair. 'Come on. I love this song.' She heard the music trip neatly into the first chorus and knew by the time she got out there it would be too far gone to enjoy it.

Harry tilted his head to the bar. 'Boy Wonder over there thinks you're a bit special. Maybe he'll dance with you.'

Emma looked up to find a semi-familiar face behind the bar. After bestowing a brief smile the bartender looked away, blushing madly.

Harry made a big show of shuffling off his chair. 'I can leave if you two would prefer to be alone.'

'No, thanks.'

'Are you sure? I can go over and tell him you love him too.'

Emma felt a certain pair of eyes swing her way. She held out a hand to stop him from going any further. 'Harry. Sit. Down.'

Harry did as he was told. 'Okay. But you just say the word…'

'I'll say two words. Shut. Up.'

'Okey dokey.'

Emma grabbed her champagne glass and downed the remainder, then refilled it herself before taking another calming sip. He was infuriating. She had forgotten how infuriating. Somehow, in her daydreams, this one characteristic seemed to fade the longer he had been away. But now she remembered—he made her itch all over.

Emma felt something brush against her foot and she all but leapt from her chair. By the time she realised it had been Harry's foot, and that he had been playing footsies under the table, it was too late. She was already tucked up on her chair with a hand to her chest to cover her adrenalin-accelerated breathing.

'What?' he said in all innocence.

Feeling embarrassed at her reaction, Emma snapped, 'Don't do that unless you mean it.'

When a bewildered look crossed his face she wished she had kept her mouth shut.

'Just a hint,' she said, before grinning inanely and popping a pretzel into her wayward mouth. 'You don't want me leaping away from you in horror every time you come near me. People might talk.'

'So you're giving hints already, are you?'

'Sure. Why not? So far we don't have to play footsies unless you mean it, and you've got to dance with your woman, for Pete's sake!'

He held his hand to his heart as he scoffed in mock outrage. 'I choose to ignore those comments until you answer this one pertinent question: how's *your* love life?'

Emma bit down on another pretzel and it crunched loudly in her mouth. Her grin faded and Harry's grew.

'That bad, huh?'

She shrugged. 'No better or worse than anybody else's, I expect. Though by your efforts on this date, better than yours, I would say.'

Harry raised one eloquent eyebrow. 'I think my efforts have been pretty darned good, thank you very much. Besides which, they aren't finished yet.'

He took up footsies with a vengeance, coming at her with such speed that she had to tuck her feet right under her chair to get away. But he was not to be deterred. He shuffled lower in his seat so that his legs sought out hers, curling around them, tugging at her until they were both half under the table.

'Hey, Emma!' a feminine voice called out.

Emma whipped her head around to spy Keely and her fiancé Lachlan, heading her way. Keely looked gorgeous in a tight Indian silk top stretched over her bump and a matching long sleek skirt.

As one she and Harry sat back up on their chairs like proper grown-ups.

Emma stood on champagne-filled legs and gave her friend a hug. She gave Lachlan a kiss on the cheek. 'What are you guys doing here?' she asked with forced brightness. 'This isn't your side of town.'

'We are heading upstairs for dinner. It's a do for Lachlan's radio station,' Keely explained. 'You guys are welcome to gatecrash if you'd like. Otherwise I know I will be cornered by Father Jerry and the crazy woman who runs the women's studies hour.' Keely held a hand tenderly over her lightly rounded belly.

'Thanks,' Emma said. 'But I think we're going to head back home to make an early night of it. It's been quite an afternoon and I'm sure Harry needs his beauty sleep.'

Harry nodded. 'I don't look like this without a lot of work.'

Emma felt a distinct kick in the shins and knew she could no longer go without introductions.

'Sorry, I forgot you hadn't met everyone. Lachlan is an eminent psychologist and has his own radio programme. Lachlan, this is my Harry.'

Harry immediately leant in to shake Lachlan's hand leaving Emma to wonder if she had actually called him *my* Harry. If so, she wished the floor would open up and swallow her right then and there.

'Nice to meet you, Emma's Harry,' Lachlan said. 'Really, if you guys wish to join us you would keep *me* from the

clutches of the depressed station manager and the nympho-
maniac receptionist.'

'I think that description comes with the position,' Keely
said with a wink, referring to WWW's own receptionist ex-
traordinaire, Chrystal, who had done her best to take on
Lachlan right under Keely's nose.

'Not tonight,' Emma said. 'Later in the week, perhaps,
without the station manager and receptionist *et al*?'

Lachlan wrapped a protective arm around Keely's waist.
'Sounds good. We'd better head on upstairs. Nice to meet
you, Harry. Emma.'

After smiles, handshakes and kisses all round Keely and
Lachlan left.

'Do you know everybody in this city?' Harry asked.

'Yes, I know *everybody*,' Emma snapped. 'That's what
comes from staying in one place for more than a year.'

Emma closed her eyes to calm herself. She opened her
eyes and shot Harry an apologetic smile. 'I think Grumpy
here really is done for the night. Is that okay?'

'Sure. Though only if you admit it was you who gave in
before I was able to prove my romantic ways to you. And
is there really a restaurant upstairs?'

Emma watched her friends disappear around the corner,
arms about one another, so in love it almost hurt to watch.
'One of the most romantic in town.'

Harry let his head fall into his palms. 'That clinches it; I
really did fail miserably.'

'Not miserably. With dignity, I would say.'

'You would say that.' Harry wrapped an arm about her
shoulder and gave her a friendly kiss on top of her head.
Emma leant to rest her head on his shoulder. It was all she
could do not to purr.

'So what went wrong?' He ran his fingers though his hair,

leaving it a dishevelled mess, and Emma had to fight the urge to tame the waves back into place. She wondered, and not for the first time, what his hair would feel like slipping through her fingers. 'Come on, lay it all on the line. I can take it.'

'Well…' she said, eking it out as long as she could as she so enjoyed watching him squirm and blush and not seem as though he had the world in the palm of his hand. 'You could have dressed up a tad more.'

He looked down at his same old same old clothes, and then back at her in shock. 'But this is me. This is Harry. I wouldn't be me without the leather and denim.'

Emma shrugged.

'What would you prefer?' he scoffed. 'A suit?'

'Sure. Why not?'

'Because I wouldn't want to come across as some kind of anal uptight executive type.'

That was enough for Emma to shoot him a two raised eyebrow look. With his windswept hair, tanned face and sunny attitude he could not come across as anal, uptight or executive without taking some kind of pill.

'It's not about looking uptight, it's about looking… together, ambitious, caring about yourself. I simply don't think that my workmates will believe that I would end up with a guy like you.'

Emma was surprised to find Harry was really mulling it over. He was actually taking her comments to heart. Harry Buchanan, heart-breaker, was concerned that she did not see him as quite the catch he imagined. Ha! If he only knew.

'They are a cute couple,' Harry said, glancing towards the stairs where Keely and her elegant Lachlan had recently gone.

'Aren't they?'

'I thought Keely knew about our deal, so why didn't you introduce me as your fiancé?'

Emma sensed a hint of…something in his voice. Disappointment? 'It's tricky,' she explained. 'Keely knows I was going to broach the idea with you but it still won't be the same with them as it will when we tell complete strangers. It will take some finessing.'

'Considering she doesn't really know me from the bartender, the idea must have shocked the heck out of her.'

Emma afforded Harry a grim smile, though she knew her friends didn't find the news as far from left field as he imagined. 'So did you tell the bartender we were engaged?' she asked.

Harry opened his mouth then snapped it shut.

'Hmm. Doesn't feel natural, does it?' she asked.

'Not yet, which is why we are here, why we will get this romance stuff down pat. Tonight was a first try, and I'm not willing to give up on us yet.'

Emma coughed back a laugh, thinking about the number of times she had soothed herself to sleep with those very words. Emma knew it would take more than 'romance stuff' for their engagement to feel right. It would take for Harry to feel as much for her as she felt for him and, though she knew he played his cards close to his chest, she was not sure that he was *that* good an actor.

'Come on, Buchanan. Time to go.'

Emma took Harry's hand to steady herself as they walked back through the dancing throng and into the cool night outside.

'I think all you proved tonight is that you need serious help. But under my tutelage you could very well become the world's greatest romantic.'

'For a girl whose only response to how her love life was

going was some serious chewing on a pretzel, you seem pretty sure of yourself.'

'Of course I am,' Emma said as they rounded on to the front path of her apartment building.

'So what are you planning to base these teachings on?' he asked.

'The greatest collection of romantic DVDs the world has ever seen.'

Snow kicked up all around Harry's snow board as he careened down the mountainside. His goggles were covered in melting wet splashes, diminishing his field of view, but that only heightened the thrill all the more.

'I dare you!' Harry grinned as the words rang in his ears. He had yelled them to his friend, the oft-sounded challenge echoing off the mountain slope, and then the race had begun.

Harry braced himself and angled his body to heighten his speed. He hadn't seen Jamie in a while and the last thing he wanted was to get to the bottom of the hill to find his best mate standing, leaning against his board, chatting up some cool blonde snow bunny and checking his watch as though he had been waiting there all day.

The ground became bumpier beneath his board, so he figured the terrain was changing up ahead. Rocks? Trees? A cliff? He shot out a foot and slowed, unsurprised when all three obstacles came suddenly into view. Angling the board at the best angle, he careened off the sloping rock, over the drop and landed easily in between the trees.

Ready to let out a whoop of exhilaration, his breath caught in his throat. The sight before him had him slamming a foot into the snow and spinning to a sudden, grinding halt.

A body. In a red ski suit. Lying crumpled and still. Wrapped around the base of a nearby pine tree.

His breath came in great cold shaking raking gulps and his heart slammed against his ribs so hard he felt faint.

'Jamie!' Harry called out, but his voice travelled no further than his lips, which were shivering more from the intense cold that had gripped his heart than from the surrounding virgin snow.

Uncurling his suddenly stiff limbs from the snow board, he somehow lifted himself to his feet, then managed to place one foot in front of the other as he made his way towards the tree, all the while willing Jamie to move, to groan, to roll towards him, laughing at his neat trick.

He found himself staring down at the lifeless form and had no idea how long he had been standing there—seconds, minutes, a lifetime—before he crouched to his knees and felt for a pulse.

But there was none.

Jamie was gone. The vibrant laughing guy who had only minutes before yelled with teenage delight as he had taken off down the mountain at breakneck speed was no longer alive.

He sank to his knees by his best friend. Tracks of salty tears warmed his icy-cold face. He whipped the now foggy goggles from his head and tossed them as far as he could, letting out a great, wracking, soul-wrenching roar that shook the snow from the tree above him.

With nobody else within calling distance, Harry took the limp body in his arms, stood, and began the slow, slippery trek down the mountain on foot, his mind whirring up to speed again as he realised what the next few hours would entail. What would he tell their friends? Jamie's parents? Jamie's little sister? Emma, oh, God!

And with each heavy step down the cold mountain his heart slowly turned to ice. He had dared Jamie to careen down the hill. Now Jamie was dead, and it was all his fault...

Harry woke with a start.

He sat up; his fist shot to his chest as though that would help stem the rampaging beat of his too-heavy heart. His whole body was slick with sweat. The sheets were tangled about him. He tore at them, untwisting the damp pink cotton from his shaking limbs and throwing them to the floor.

He slid his feet to the floor and braced his elbow on his knees. He shot a hunted glance at his faintly glowing wrist-watch. It was three in the morning. He had managed three hours of solid sleep before the dream took a hold.

Running hot, shaking palms over his face, he collected his runaway breath.

It was okay. He was not alone. He was in Melbourne. Emma was across the hall. But, no matter the comfort that brought, the dream would return. It was the one week of the year in which he could not stand to be alone, no matter how much he deserved nothing less.

CHAPTER FIVE

EMMA'S CHOICE VIDEO NIGHT YEARS BEFORE
'So if a woman asks a man to dance what she really
wants is to do the horizontal tango? Wow. That snippet
would have saved me a lot of time in the past,'
said Harry, before receiving a well-aimed cushion
to the head from Emma during Dirty Dancing.

ON WEDNESDAY morning Emma left Harry to sleep off the champagne of the night before. She tiptoed into his room and left a note atop his leather jacket saying to meet her at work later in the morning. A pink sheet barely covered his body, his feet sticking out over the end of her childhood bed. She didn't know whether she wanted to whip off the sheet and find out whether he wore as little to bed as she had always imagined or to tickle those adorable curling toes. Realising the tickle would probably have achieved both ends, she shot out of the room.

She met the girls at Sammy's, a quaint little coffee shop-cum-noodle bar below a string of high rises near their work place in Southbank.

As usual, Emma arrived early and Tahlia dead on time. Tradition was further upheld when Keely arrived late, her arms filled with wedding magazines and *Keely's Collection*, her ever-present scrapbook, filled with notes and ideas about how to have a perfect life which she had collected since she was a kid.

'Sorry, sorry,' Keely gushed. 'Lachlan kept me kind of busy all morning—'

'Ooh, Keely, come on!' Tahlia cried. 'Remember we talked about this. Too much information!'

Keely shrugged, slapped her magazines on to the table, then turned and grabbed Emma by the upper arms. 'You have no idea how hard it was not to ask when I saw you last night—how did your little spider and fly trap go? Are you and your Harry officially engaged?'

Emma took a deep breath and dived in. 'We are.'

Andy, their regular waiter, arrived at that moment with their breakfast of fresh fruit, yoghurt and cappuccinos. But Keely squealed, her arms flung out in excitement, and poor Andy ended up covered in fresh fruit, yoghurt and cappuccinos.

'Oh, Andy, I am so-o-o-o sorry!' Keely cried. 'I was a klutz before, but when you add baby brain to the mix there are no bounds to my clumsiness.'

All three girls took to wiping the young man down with handfuls of paper napkins but they only seemed to create a worse mess.

'Don't sweat it, Ms Rhodes,' Andy said, backing away from their clamouring palms. 'I'll bring you another serve right away.'

'Are you sure? Okay. Thanks, Andy.'

Once Andy was inside, the girls cracked up laughing.

'Don't!' Keely yelled. 'If I laugh any more I'm going to pee my pants! I have no control over anything any more. This little one has taken away all of my basic faculties.'

Emma brushed away tears from her cheeks. 'We must have looked like three desperate women taking every chance to give the poor guy a touch up.'

'I know!' Tahlia chimed in. 'I'm sure at one stage I was

wiping over his butt, and the food was only over his front. I am a sad, sad woman.'

'What's with all that Ms Rhodes stuff?' Keely asked. 'You'd think I was ten years older than him.'

'You almost are!' Emma said. 'He's got to be eighteen. Nineteen at the most.'

'Nevertheless a truly beautiful work of art,' Tahlia said on a sigh.

'Though he looked more like a work of *modern* art covered in all that multi-coloured food!' Emma added.

Their laughter eased to sporadic giggles and they each sat back clutching their aching stomachs.

'Now,' Tahlia said, 'what were we talking about?'

'Emma!' Keely shouted, 'and the clever way she finagled her way into becoming engaged to the love of her life.'

Emma's laughter died away and she drew her hands to her now blushing face. 'Keely, you know that's not how it is. I am just doing him a favour. Nobody in Melbourne knows him well enough now to know any different so it should be easy enough.'

'Of course it should. For him,' Keely said. 'Though why does he think you have gone along with it? Even if you didn't declare your undying love, the guy is going to begin to wonder.'

Emma fluffed a hand to brush off their questions. There was no way she could tell them Harry had agreed to come on board with WWW Designs, not right on top of her latest news. They would figure out why. They were too clever for their own good. No, that news had to come later. The last thing she wanted was for her gorgeous friends to fret over their jobs. She would look after everything. Smooth-things-over Emma. Fixer-upper Emma. Good-girl Emma.

'I am a little afraid of scamming the good people of *Flirt* magazine by doing it, though,' she tossed out, drawing their attention to a new line of thinking.

'*Flirt*, schmirt,' Keely insisted. 'By the looks of the other guys, they'll do fine. Though I must admit, that man of yours would have been in with a real chance.'

'He's not my man,' Emma insisted.

'For now, he is, my young friend. Now it's up to you to decide what to do with him.'

Tahlia reached into her massive handbag and grabbed a torn-out page from a magazine. 'After we chatted about your plan last night, I checked on your stars. No harm in taking advice from every avenue possible, right? So here goes: *"Leo. You find you can't ignore what others can hardly see. You wish you could turn a blind eye. Life would be much easier. Your only option now is to put it right."'* Tahlia nodded sagely then tucked the page back into her bag. 'Makes sense to me. Follow your instinct and help Harry.'

The words tumbled over in Emma's mind but she saw a different angle entirely. Help Tahlia. Help Keely. Help WWW Designs. Either way, according to Madame Zuta, she was on the right track.

Andy arrived with their replacement breakfast. He wore a clean shirt and gave a wide berth to *Ms Rhodes*. He shot the girls a small smile then left.

'First things first; I have to introduce him to Raquel. He called his contact at *Flirt* last night with the news and he's going to meet me here when I give the news to Raquel. Better she finds out from me than from the client.'

Keely's lip curled. 'You'd better sharpen your claws first, my sweet. That woman is pure beast. After you left yesterday she went on a rampage through the offices, spouting the end of the world is nigh mantras.'

'Pfft,' Tahlia scoffed. 'That's just her usual schtick to

keep us all in line. WWW is doing great. I've lined up two massive new clients already this week.'

Before Emma gave in to the urge to tell the girls about her odd conversation with Raquel the day before, and the damning legal letter burning a hole in her briefcase, Chrystal—WWW's receptionist, gossip and office tart— walked past, wearing the same clothes from the day before.

'You been home yet, Chrystal?' Keely asked, her tongue firmly in her cheek.

'Are you kidding?' Chrystal replied before slumping into a seat next to them. 'I don't think I have slept on a Tuesday night in three years. Ladies' night,' she explained.

'Any luck?' Tahlia asked.

'Some. None.' She shook her head, red curls slapping across her face. 'But it's all good. Tonight I will sleep and dream of bigger and better men to come.' With a great tragic sigh, Chrystal heaved herself from the chair and tottered off on heels so high her knees were perpetually bent.

'She's trouble on two legs, that one,' Keely said.

'I don't know,' Tahlia said. 'I think she is in the same boat as the rest of us. She is just searching in a different way.'

Keely was obviously not convinced, but Emma heard the feather-light touch of desolation in her other friend's voice. She well knew that feeling, when life hit a point where a girl had to do what a girl had to do...

Emma gave her friend a one-armed hug. 'Tahlia, Tahlia, always the sensitive one.'

'So what does that make me? Insensitive?' Keely asked over the top of a bridal magazine.

'That makes you the engaged one, so you no longer count.'

Keely looked ready to fire back, but then she sort of

melted, her face coming over all soft and sweet as the reality sank in. 'I am the engaged one. Really engaged. Properly engaged. I can scarce believe my luck.'

Emma shifted in her seat and felt Tahlia doing the same.

'Now, I think I have found the dress,' Keely said from nowhere.

Emma, her mind numbed by the evenly weighted happiness and envy she felt towards her friend's newfound and wholly requited love, said 'What dress?'

'The-e-e-e dress. My wedding dress.'

Tahlia gave Emma a pinch on the arm. 'Of course we knew you meant *the-e-e-e* dress, we just want you to show us.'

Keely glared at her for a moment before giving in and believing her.

Emma sat back in her chair and gave in to the guilty pleasure of talk about tulle versus satin and arguments over how much one should spend on a pair of wedding shoes one would never wear again, knowing the hangover of regret she would experience later in the day when she came back down to earth to realise there was very great doubt such luck in love would ever fall her way.

An hour later, Emma waited with Harry in Raquel's assistant Penelope's office.

Penelope beamed as they entered. 'Emma! So nice to see you,' she said, her 's's lost within an obvious lisp. 'Raquel won't be too long.'

'Which actually means we'll probably have to wait a while,' Emma explained to Harry. 'She's notorious for making people wait to show how important she is.'

She winked at Penelope, who grinned back, nodding in agreement. Emma then sat, thinking that even Penelope, sweet-natured Penelope, with her shy nature and speech impediment, had landed herself a gorgeous guy to call her own. No wonder she managed to work for Raquel without developing a rash or a drinking habit.

When Penelope left her office for a moment, Emma took the chance to grab the lost letter and slip it into a pile of paper on Penelope's desk, knowing if Raquel had ever found out it had been out of her assistant's possession she would have torn the girl into a million pieces. Having the document out of her hands meant one less spinning plate to worry about.

Harry prowled about the office like a caged cat. He fiddled with leaves on the big potted palm in the corner, peered out the window to the Yarra River far below, and played with a stack of Post-It Notes.

'You are making me nervous,' Emma hissed. 'Can't you just be still?'

'Actually, no. I can't. Being still makes *me* nervous, so I guess if one of us has to be nervous, it can be you.'

She glared at him and he glared right back. The sparks flinting off the two of them could set the room alight.

Raquel's dismembered voice called through the speaker box on Penelope's desk. 'Penny, tell Ms Radfield I'll give her two minutes.'

Penelope still hadn't returned but Emma headed to the door nonetheless. She poked a finger at Harry. 'Stay.'

He held his paws in front of him and panted like a puppy so Emma entered Raquel's office wearing a grin.

'What is it, Ms Radfield?' Raquel demanded before she had even shut the door. 'I'm seriously busy right now.'

Emma's grin disappeared. She set her teeth, knowing that when she told her boss her news she would be treated with the respect she deserved. 'I have some good news, Raquel.'

'If you tell me that you have discovered a new name for the colour red you are so partial to in your little paintings, I don't want to hear about it.'

Emma sincerely thought about walking out then and there, taking Harry's business with her. But then she thought of Keely, with her wedding plans and a baby on the way, and of Tahlia, so hanging on for the much deserved promotion. No, she had to stay.

'No new name for red, Raquel. But I have managed to convince Harry Buchanan to bring the design and management of *Harold's House* under the wing of WWW Designs.'

Raquel's face paled and, though no words were forthcoming, Emma felt a chill. She knew then that the rescue plan was more important than she had even guessed and that she may have found the very lifeline they needed.

'You mean to bring him here?' Raquel asked.

'I thought that would work best for us.'

'But we have nowhere to house such a huge client.'

Jeez. For a woman who sure needed this, she was making it hard for Emma to do her a favour. 'Well, I was thinking upstairs.'

Raquel's voice dimmed to a horrified whisper. 'You can't mean the dump.'

Emma counted to ten under her breath. 'As far as I recall, it's only full of old furniture and dust bunnies. With a good clean and a lick of paint it will be a fantastic and private space for them to run the business, as well as giving our design and sales teams easy access.'

Raquel began to nod, slowly, but enough for Emma to know she was latching on to the idea, so she jumped in boots and all. 'Raquel, I am up to date with my current projects, so I would be happy to oversee the clean up.'

Raquel small nod became effusive. 'Great. Right.' She

flapped a sharply taloned hand in Emma's face. 'You can take care of all that. Wow. *Harold's House* joining with *my* company. I knew I still had it in me.'

Counting to ten no longer helped. Emma had to pinch her own thigh to stop herself from screaming out, or laughing maniacally, or just plain quitting. 'Harry Buchanan is outside right now if you would like to meet him,' she said.

'He is?' Raquel's hand flew to a mirror compact in her top drawer and she frantically puffed and preened. 'Well, go on! Bring him in, then.'

So ordered, Emma walked to the door. She popped her head around to find Harry flicking a table lamp on and off and shot Penelope a sorry smile. Penelope grinned back.

'Come on, *Harold*,' Emma said, 'you're on.'

Harry's mouth kicked up on one side, sending Emma's heart rate skittering. She turned on her heel and he followed, sauntering in behind her.

'Raquel, I assume,' he said, his voice exuding latent charm. He reached to shake Emma's boss's fluttering hand.

'Harry. I hear that you find our little operation appealing.'

'And then some,' he said, taking a seat beside Emma.

'What extra luck,' Raquel continued, 'as you are one of the star nominees in *Flirt*'s Australia's Hunkiest Bloke competition. I know it's fairly late notice but we have a few days before Saturday night's big decision to promote the hell out of your move and nomination in the press. You are a slam dunk, my friend!'

Emma felt Harry seize up beside her. 'Um, actually, Raquel, Harry is no longer able to participate in *Flirt*'s comp.'

Raquel turned on Emma, the Rottweiler nickname coming into full force. 'Why the hell not?'

Emma flinched—her boss's words were so full of

venom—but then Harry's hand slipped on to her knee and she felt instantly shielded, protected.

'Because my recent engagement makes me ineligible to participate,' he said, his voice coming out as deep as a growl. He may as well have yelled at her to back off.

Raquel blinked, the tone stopping her short, and then her beady eyes narrowed, focusing on Harry's stern face and the position of his hand. Finally her gaze slithered back up to Emma's face. 'He's engaged?' she asked, her eyebrows disappearing under her heavy fringe. 'To you?'

Emma hadn't really thought about putting it into practice, about what to say to people other than her friends who were in the know as to the whys and hows. Now that Raquel knew, the world would be put on notice. So she baulked. Until Harry gave her knee a little squeeze. He needed her to do this.

'I am,' Emma said, then cleared her throat to dislodge the lump within. 'We are. Engaged. To each other.'

'So what? He couldn't afford a rock?' Raquel said with disdain.

Emma looked down at her bare hand.

'The ring was my grandmother's,' Harry said before Emma even had a chance to think of an excuse to cover that huge blunder. 'It's being resized. Em's fingers are so dainty whereas Nanna had fingers as thick as sausages.'

Emma could do little but smile and nod in agreement.

Raquel sat back in her chair, her fingers meeting like a church steeple beneath her chin. 'Well, well, well. Sweet little Emma Radfield with big, bad Harry Buchanan. It's always the quiet ones who shock you most.'

Emma could do nothing but smile back, though her teeth ground behind her thinned lips.

'So, no *Flirt* nomination then. Pity. But I simply can't let this wonderful news slide on by regardless. Let me throw a wham bam engagement party for you. We'll grab a room at the Ivy and put on a real show.'

Oh, God! Raquel's sort of wham bam would mean press and unrecognisable party food and people they had never met. Harry's hand tightened painfully on her knee, but she was way ahead of him.

'Sorry, Raquel, but Tahlia and Keely have already organised one for us. Thanks for your kind offer, but you'll hear more when the date is set. Okay?'

Emma's mind raced. She would have to get on to the girls before Raquel could, and to have them organise a bloody party. And she would have to do it ASAP!

Emma stood, dragging Harry with her. 'Okay, Raquel, Harry has to be elsewhere, so if you wouldn't mind getting on to the contracts with Harry's business manager—' that will keep her busy for a good hour, Emma thought '—that would be fab.'

She threw Harry's business manager's card on to Raquel's desk then tore from the room before Raquel could contradict her.

Harry barely waited until they were out of earshot. 'What on earth is this about a party? I never said anything about a party!'

'Tough,' Emma said as she barrelled through the hallway, frantically text messaging Keely in shorthand.

meet me@ T's in 5

'It was either play meet the press for Raquel or control the damage using Tahlia and Keely, okay?' she said.

'Okay, then. Jeez. No need to be so snippy.'

Emma slowed. She took a deep, calming breath. 'Sorry. I guess I'm just feeling a little nervy right now.' Emma knew she couldn't organise all that needed to be organised in front of Harry. The girls would give her away in a second. 'Why don't you take the morning for yourself? You'll need to get on to your key people about moving in here. Chrystal can find you a spare office with a phone or you can use the one at home and I'll meet you for lunch, okay? It'll be great. I can show you my Melbourne.'

'I was born here.'

She sent her message and looked up at him, her whole body humming with frustration, but she held on tight, keeping her half a dozen spinning plates balanced high above her head while walking the added tightrope that was her relationship with Harry.

'It was a joke, Harry. Now, go. Meet me back here at two o'clock and we'll go from there.'

Her phone rang, the *Copacabana* tune blaring out sweetly into the silence. It was Keely. Emma switched her phone off. Her friend would have to wait.

'You have an unhealthy addiction to Barry Manilow,' Harry said.

'That song breaks my heart and you can dance to it. What more could one want?'

'As far as I remember it's a cautionary tale, warning people not to fall in love.'

'So it is.' Emma could tell Harry was dragging his feet, and it only added to the ache in her chest, thinking that he would prefer to stay with her than do anything else.

'Two o'clock,' he said, pointing at her as though burning the time into her memory.

'Two o'clock,' she promised, grabbing him by the jacket, spinning him about and shoving him down the hall.

When he was gone she slumped against the wall, the last of her energy threatening to up and leave her. But she had too much to do before two o'clock. She had to break the good news about *Harold's House* to her friends as though it was new news, she had to line up a team to help her get the top floor in order for *Harold's House*'s people, she had to organise a fake engagement party, she had to photocopy her Blondie presentation for a meeting with a bigwig from *Flirt*, and she had to do all of that with the scent *à la* Harry still lingering about her.

It was almost too much for one girl to bear. But this was a girl who had long since learned how to keep everyone happy at once.

She slipped into her office, slumped into her chair, clicked open her web browser and, as she had told Harry, *Harold's House* opened as her home page.

Instantly distracted, she nibbled on a fingernail, staring at the background—a swirl of browns, reds and greys so indicative of the Australian outback. A large house stood, stately and inviting, in the middle of the screen. All she had to do was click a window-pane, the doorknob, the weather-vane, and she would be transported into one of a million different worlds.

But she simply stared at the house, *Harold's House*, which was, in fact, a near perfect replica of the house she had grown up in. The house in which Harry, after long since noticing her secret sketches, had quietly presented her with her first set of paintbrushes. The house in which she had first cried on Harry's welcoming shoulder after a boy at school she liked had called her brace face. The house in which they had spent a dozen birthdays, a half dozen Christmases and, a decade prior, one wake.

So if this house, this place, her family, her memories,

their shared history, meant so much to him, was so much a part of him that he presented it to the world as his heart and soul, what made it so easy or so necessary for him to leave? Time and time again?

More than ever before, Emma found herself determined to find out.

Emma finished off the colourful, kitsch, kaleidoscopic presentation of Australia's Hunkiest Bloke nominees, minus the page about one Harry Buchanan, to some very happy representatives of *Flirt* magazine.

'Superb,' gushed Marcie, the elegant Managing Director of *Flirt*. She took Emma aside while the rest of the gang filed out of the room towards post-meeting coffee and biscuits.

'Thanks, Marcie. That means a lot coming from you.'

Marcie nodded, knowing it to be true. 'It seems you are a woman of many talents. I hear you're the one who took our favourite bloke out of the competition?'

Emma stood straight and tall to stop herself from fidgeting under the clear, knowing gaze. 'Harry was favourite?' she asked, feeling all the more guilty for that fact. So much for making sure everyone else was happy.

'You should be the last to be surprised by that fact, my sweet.'

Emma smiled. 'Too true.'

'You only became engaged in the last couple of days. Is that correct?'

Emma bit her lip. 'Mm-hmm.'

'But they have known each other for ever,' Keely interjected, bumbling into the conversation, licking icing sugar from her top lip. 'It's adorable. They are so in love they even make me jealous!'

Marcie didn't take her eyes off Emma the whole time. 'Is that so?' Marcie leaned backward resting her bony backside against the kitchenette bench and watching Emma with such intensity that Emma feared the woman would be able to imbibe her soul if she so desired.

'So tell me about it.'

'Not for the magazine…' Emma said, knowing the last thing Harry would want would be the adverse publicity his engagement might bring on. 'Since Harry has nothing to do with your competition, I don't see how it matters.'

Marcie gave an elegant shrug. 'Fine. Not for *Flirt*. Just for me. Give an old married broad a thrill. Tell me your love story.'

Emma swallowed hard and looked to Keely who was as encouraging as she could be without shouting, *Just do it, Em!* Emma licked her lips and tried to come up with a story, any story, but the only thought filling her mind was the truth.

'We met when I was eleven. He was fifteen.'

'Ah. He was captain of the footy team I suppose.'

Emma shook her head. 'No. That was Jamie.'

'Jamie?'

'My older brother.'

Emma kept her eyes glued to Marcie, knowing that by now Keely would be more than interested in her story. The girls knew she'd had a brother who had died young, but had picked up on Emma's signals not to probe too deep. It was simply something she had not found the capacity to talk about with those who didn't know him. Feeling Keely's concerned eyes on her, she clung to the story replaying itself in her mind.

'Harry was not captain material. He was too much of a wild card. He was the guy who came up with plays the coach would never have considered. And he was also the only one of Jamie's friends who gave me the time of day.' *More than the time of day,* she thought. *He gave me friendship, advice, a shoulder to cry on, a helping hand, the confidence to draw, the strength to keep my family whole once Jamie was...*

'So,' Marcie encouraged, 'was it love at first sight?'

Emma nodded her head. 'Without a doubt.' For *me anyway*, Emma thought.

Marcie laughed. Then, after a few silent moments, she said, 'Hmm. I can see why. He is a handsome devil.'

Keely made a sharp mewling sound which caught Emma's attention. Keely bobbed her head towards the doorway. Emma followed the direction of her friend's gaze to find Harry standing outside the office, chatting to Chrystal who as usual was twirling a red curl around her finger and giggling loudly.

As though sensing a roomful of women looking his way, Harry turned. When he *found* a roomful of women looking his way he grinned his irresistible, all-Australian-male grin, and Emma felt the round of swoons buffet against her back.

Catching her eye, his grin broadened, deepened, lit up his face, then softened into an apologetic smile. He tapped his watch, pointed to the ground intimating he would meet her downstairs, shot the room a sexy salute then went back to his conversation with Chrystal, who was by that time bouncing about in front of him doing her best to recapture his attention.

Marcie waggled a finger at Emma, whose heart was slamming through her chest at how close she had come to putting her foot in her mouth. If Harry had heard her words...he would have thought it was part of the act. Of course he would.

'I won't forgive you for depriving our readers of that delicious specimen, Ms Radfield. I salute you, but I don't forgive you.'

Her heart rate returning to a more normal pace, Emma sent back what she hoped was a sorry smile. 'I just hope the presentation more than makes up for losing Harry,' she said.

'It's perfect. Better than even I could have imagined. Your animation of the perpetually swooning girl in the bottom corner of the frame gives such a fantastic through line to the whole reel. She's just lovely and so perfectly indicative of the winsome feel we wanted for the competition.'

'I am so glad to hear that. She was a real joy to play with. Now, Marcie, if you don't mind, I have another engagement, so to speak.' Emma felt a strange sort of blush rise up her throat at the words and hoped Marcie would think it was because she was bashful and in love, not because she hated lying to the woman at her side. 'Do call, email, anything if you have any last-minute concerns. I'll be happy to take any of your ideas on board.'

'Do you mind if I walk you to the lift?' Marcie asked, and how could Emma say no? The woman was a legend. A maker of careers. A builder of media empires. And someone who was about to challenge her on her lie?

'Sure,' she said and tried to look nonchalant while Keely jumped up and down and clapped silently.

As Marcie joined Emma in the lift she asked, 'So now that we have no friends and acquaintances listening in, tell me, this thing between you and the Wunderkind, is it for real?'

Emma thought of Harry's pale face when contemplating any sort of involvement with *Flirt* and its sort. 'I'm afraid it is,' Emma said, letting all her love for him shine forth. 'So you can't have him.'

'It isn't *him* that I want.'

'Excuse me?' Emma said, stepping out of the lift and into the marble ground floor foyer. Her gaze was invariably drawn outside. Through the glass doors she could see Harry leaning against his motorbike. Alone. A loner in denim and leather.

'Ms Radfield,' Marcie said, trying to reclaim Emma's attention. She held the door open and pinned Emma to the spot with her steely-eyed gaze. 'I have every intention of attempting to head-hunt you away from this outfit.'

'Me? What…whatever for?'

'Your work has made waves at our parent company.'

'In New York?'

'Mmm. In New York. Your past work is the main reason WWW got this gig, my sweet. You draw like a master and your animation is fluid, easy and eye-catching. We feel the congeniality and youthfulness of your characters would bring the stuffy image of our parent and subsidiary companies into the twenty-first century.'

Emma's heart slammed against her ribs, knocked itself out, landed deep in her chest cavity, awoke and returned to its usual programming. Marcie ran not only *Flirt* but a range of magazines, newspapers, several highly rated and diverse cable television networks overseas. The scope for her work would be unequalled. 'But that would mean my having to move to…'

'To New York.' The lift door began to beep. 'I'm heading up to talk to your…boss.' Marcie's face showed exactly what she thought of the blustery Raquel. 'But I'll keep this conversation between us. Okay?'

Emma nodded vehemently.

'Think about it, won't you? I'll chat to you again at the party on Saturday night, by which time I hope we can begin to talk specifics.'

All Emma could promise was, 'No worries,' though for the first time in her life she didn't even believe herself when she said it.

Marcie slid her hand away from the metal door and disappeared into the shadows as the heavy doors closed.

Emma walked out into the weak spring sunshine having added an extra spinning plate to her act.

CHAPTER SIX

GIRLS' NIGHT IN WITH **TITANIC**
'She'd begged him not to go. Yet off he went, never to be seen again. Typical man,' Emma screamed to the heavens. Keely linked arms and brought her back to earth. 'Em, I don't think you can really equate Harry going to Uluru with Leo DiCaprio drowning in the Atlantic.'

SNUGGLED up against Harry on the back of his motorbike, Emma directed him to *her Melbourne*, which meant clothes shopping on Chapel Street.

'You weren't kidding about making me buy new gear, were you?' Harry groaned as he hopped off the bike.

'Nope. If you are going to play at being my fiancé, you will have to dress the part. Especially now there is going to be a party tomorrow night'

'That soon?'

'That soon. Unless you want Raquel to have time to book herself a room at the Ivy, call the press, file her claws...'

Harry slapped a hand over Emma's mouth. 'Okay, pip-squeak. I get your point.' Emma poked out her tongue against his palm and Harry pulled his hand away. 'Eww!'

'You're losing your touch, Buchanan. You should have seen that one coming.'

'Watch out, Em. There's payback coming your way.'

Emma bit down on her lip. What was she doing baiting him like that? He was the king of pranks. The master of payback. A world-renowned daredevil. She chose to simply ignore him.

'Then there is the *Flirt* do on Saturday night,' she continued.

'Are you actually thinking of going?' he asked. Again she heard the same vulnerable shade to his voice as when she had told him that her parents had gone away.

'Of course. I'm super proud of my work on this project and I would like to be there to see it all come together. I was kind of hoping that even though you're no longer involved you might come too.' She didn't mention her promise to meet with Marcie there. It was still too fresh in her mind, too raw, too impossible to voice out loud.

'But it's on Saturday, Em. Saturday is, you know, the anniversary.'

Did he really think she had forgotten? 'I know what *Saturday* is, Harry. I thought that afternoon we would do something special for Jamie. Just the two of us. But that night is important to me too. I don't see why I can't fit both into my life.'

Harry baulked. Hard. She knew that if she begged he would capitulate, but the last thing she wanted to do was beg her *fiancé* to escort her anywhere, especially when it was so obvious he was conflicted. He was always conflicted when it came to this day.

Ten years on. That Saturday it would be ten years to the day since Jamie's accident, yet even her parents had given themselves permission to enjoy a holiday. Emma had given herself permission to attend a work function which she had every intention of enjoying. Jamie would have been thrilled to see her work up on a big screen. He would have been there in a tux with a spinning red bow-tie if he'd had half a chance. But not Harry. It seemed he wasn't giving himself permission to do anything much.

'Relax, hotshot,' she said. 'I've gone stag before and I can do so again. But, as for tomorrow night's engagement party, you are coming with me and we are going to find you an outfit fit for a man in love.'

Relax he did. At being let off the hook his whole body unclenched. Sheesh. She had had no idea the guy was wound so tight. Cool Harry Buchanan was not so cool after all.

'I was hoping to do something else today,' he said, his colour now fully returned.

Emma crossed her arms. 'And what was that?'

'Maybe the Melbourne Zoo. Or watch Collingwood footy club train. And I haven't been to a dentist in a while.'

'Harold Buchanan, you are a complete mystery to me. Don't they say to dress for the job you want and not for the job you have?'

'What makes you think I'm not doing exactly that?'

Emma knew there was more than cheeky humour behind his voice. Things were starting to form a disconcerting pattern. The months spent in Alice Springs, in Cape York, at the far tip of Tasmania. The aversion to any publicity even before he had acquired himself a dangerous fan. Was Harry really not thrilled to be such a success? Did it have something to do with the burden of grief he carried around on his shoulders?

Emma tucked the questions away for later. 'Okay, then. In a perfect world, what would you like to do when you grow up?'

That brought a smile back to her friend's lovely mouth. 'You don't think I'm grown-up yet?' He puffed out his chest and Emma had to swallow down her entirely visceral re-action to his very grown-up physique.

She turned and headed down the street towards her fa-vourite menswear shops and he followed. 'Mmm. I'm not really sure.'

'Why?'

'Well, for one thing, you don't seem terribly settled. You have no home base, you aren't entirely consumed by your job and, as far as I can tell, there is no woman in your life. You are like no other grown-up guy I know.'

Harry grabbed Emma around the waist and all but lifted her from the ground. He continued tickling her as he used to, his strength always outweighing her own. 'I'll have you know there is one woman I am very proud to have in my life.'

'Harry, come on. You know what I mean. You have no one with whom you would really want to settle down. To stay put. In one place. To make a home. To have kids.'

The tickling stopped but Harry kept his arm around her waist as they continued their stroll down the footpath. Unwilling and unable to stop herself, she slipped her arm around his waist and savoured the close contact.

'Harry, once this week is over, what then?' she asked, but even she didn't want to know the answer.

Finally he shrugged. 'You know what, princess, I have not one clue.'

Emma stopped walking and turned so she was facing her friend down. 'That's what I figured.'

Harry reached out and tucked a strand of her hair behind her ear. Her skin vibrated from her neck to her toes and if she didn't know better she would have thought he was play-ing her in order to ease her off track.

'Of course you did,' he said. 'You always were smart beyond your years.'

That did it. The whole kid sister thing. She had lived with it for years but enough was enough. 'Harry, do you have any idea how old I am?'

He opened his mouth to answer, then closed his eyes as he silently calculated.

'I'm twenty-four, you big dope.'

'No wonder your wrinkles are looking like they are there to stay.'

She ignored his teasing and stuck to the subject. 'I've seen enough, done enough, been around enough to know when a friend is at a low point and you, my friend, are so low right now it's scaring me.'

Harry stepped back. He actually took a huge step away and Emma knew she was on to something. She reached out and grabbed him by the arm.

'Harry, what are you running away from?'

At that moment a line of motorbikes drove past. Harry turned to watch them glide along the road and even Emma's gaze was drawn to the guttural noise.

She flicked a glance back to her friend and could tell he was biting at the inside of his cheek. Something in his far-away gaze told her that if he had his way he would prefer to be riding away with them rather than answering her question. The thought of him leaving again, and soon, hurt so much she had to push it to the back of her mind. She tugged on his arm, feeling like the little sister type she hated being.

'What's up?' she asked, tempting fate.

'The third one along has a great sound. I was just thinking about how they got that grunt.'

She had lost him. There would be no way of getting the conversation back to where it had been. Not then, anyway.

'The third one along?' she asked, looking to the two dozen bikes heading up the road. 'How on earth can you tell which one sounds like which?'

'Spend enough time on one, you get to know.'

Harry pulled out the regular handful of scrap papers and pencil from the top pocket of his shirt and began making notes. He'd always been like that. Organised but in such a way that nobody else would be able to make sense of his methods. As a kid, with his ubiquitous pencil and scrap paper, he would map out regular raids of the nearby battery hen farm at the beginning of the school holidays—from the distraction of the tired old security guard to the infiltration of the grounds, the pilfering of a couple of dozen good-sized eggs, all the way to the massive egg fights that would then ensue against the other local kids who had never made it into their tight little gang of three. Yet once the kids had scattered, nobody would ever have been able to pin down that it was him from his scribbles which were written in engineering language so sophisticated for a then fifteen-year-old.

Emma grabbed him by the jacket sleeve and dragged him into a menswear shop. She blithely ignored his accompanying groan. 'Come on, darling heart, it's *me* time.'

Harry tucked his pen and paper back into the safety of his top pocket and did as he was told. Emma held up an outfit any Melbourne guy would be happy to be seen wearing in any pub in town, especially in swanky St Kilda.

Harry flinched. 'You want me to try on a creased pink shirt that not only reflects light but also is meant to look like it has never been ironed, along with tight white trousers?'

'You don't like them?'

Harry glared at her, wide-eyed.

'Well, then, you've obviously been out of a big city for way too long. It's the age of the *metrosexual*, my friend. Men these days dress well. They manicure. They pedicure. They spend time on their hair.' She glanced at his natural, too-long, sun-kissed shock of hair. True, most of those men would spend hours trying to get their hair looking exactly like his, but she wasn't telling him that.

'I'd be lynched if I took one step outside in that get-up. Kids would point and laugh, men would back up against walls as I pass, and women, oh, the women…'

Emma knew the exact words he would never be able to resist, the words her illustrious older brother would utter, that had led Harry to create elaborate egg-stealing plans in the first place. 'I dare you.'

For the briefest of brief moments, Harry's face blanched of all colour. His face swam before her, cold and clammy and petrified, until he reached out, grabbed the ensemble from Emma's hands and disappeared into a cubicle.

Emma stared at the swaying curtain in silence. Low didn't begin to describe Harry's state. Whatever was going on behind those usually smiling hazel eyes was entirely beyond her powers of deduction. But that didn't mean that he was beyond her help.

Emma wandered through the shop, touching fabrics and trying not to think about Harry disrobing only metres away. Instead, she let her mind wander to that night, a couple of years before, when Harry had come to Melbourne for his yearly jaunt, and the beginnings of *Harold's House* had made their way into his top pocket.

Late one very particular night, sitting on a familiar lawn, leaning against a park bench, looking at a very particular slab of marble, engraved with one very particular young man's name, they had talked for hours on end. They had talked about that young man who would grow no older, about what he would have been doing with his life had he not been killed so suddenly several years before. About her brother and Harry's best friend. About Jamie.

'He would have been Prime Minister,' Harry had guessed. 'Or maybe a stuntman in the movies. Or the first man on Mars.'

'Nah,' Emma disagreed. 'He would have been married with seven kids by now. He would have been head of the PTA, and would have spent many a meeting standing behind the podium, ranting and raving about the lack of children specific content on the Internet.'

Harry had laughed, not aloud, but enough to show he agreed. 'Ever the one to discover a conundrum, he would then have come to me, "the man with the plan", to solve the problem for him, the PTA, and his seven kids.'

Emma had rolled her sleepy head to one side and stared at Harry, resisting the urge to run a finger along his beautiful moonlit profile.

'You would have done it for him, wouldn't you, Harry?'

Harry had then rolled his head towards her and stared right back. 'Always.'

Emma remembered the moment so clearly. Her breath had caught in her throat. Her chest had felt heavy. Her toes had tingled as all the blood in her body had rushed back to her heart. She had thought, in the moonlight, in the peace and quiet, surrounded by the comforting texture of memories and the compelling weave of what ifs, that her Harry had been about to kiss her.

After several heady moments where the only sound louder than the beat of her heart was the light wind rustling the bushes, he had grinned his lopsided grin and said, 'I would have done anything he asked. Just as he would have for me.'

'Mmm. He would have, you know. He looked up to you so much.'

Harry had scoffed and turned away and the moment had been lost, dissolved, fluttered away with the wind. She had continued to watch his throat working as he stared into the distance, past Jamie's glowing white tombstone and into the darkness beyond. Even with the half view of his eyes, she knew that a great deal of that darkness had soaked into Harry's soul. Emma's favourite person in the entire world still lived below the glossy depths of his deep hazel eyes, but it took a lot more those days to find him, to draw him out to play.

Finally something had clicked in Harry that night, and he had reached into his top pocket, gathered his mismatched scrap papers together and began to write. And write. And write.

'Are you going to tell me what you are concocting there?' Emma had asked. 'Should the children of the local area be worried?'

'On the contrary. I figure it's about time to pay them back for the years of torment we put them through.'

Emma liked to think that in that small, quiet moment, *Harold's House*, an entirely altruistic creation that had brought levity, innocence and wonder to the world, had been born.

'Emma?'

Harry's voice cut into her thoughts, and she turned from a rack of belts to find him standing in front of the large mirror at the back of the store.

She'd been joking when she had chosen the outfit, but even in his crinkly pink shirt and tight white trousers he looked unbelievably masculine. His suntanned skin glowed under the pastel clothes, his strong legs made the stretch fabric of the trousers taut. If he had worn the outfit on a billboard poster outside the store, the range would sell out in a day, most likely bought up by women hoping their men would scrub up such a treat as her Harry.

He stood with his hands clenched at his sides, his bare brown feet, with his decidedly non-pedicured toenails, scrunching into the carpet, his teeth working at his bottom lip, and Emma knew that if she told him she loved the outfit he would buy it, and wear it, to please her. That was why he looked so pained. He was preparing himself to go through social hell, just for her.

Why? Why was he so ready to be there for her this week every year? Because they were best friends? Because he knew she needed him? Or because he needed her? Her heart all but broke. He was too sweet, and utterly infuriating, and emotionally unreachable, while so obviously looking to her as the only one he could truly count on. Well, she had no plans to let him down either.

'What do you think?' she asked, prolonging the agony.

'I'm not quite sure. Is it a fancy dress party?'

Emma bit back a laugh. 'No. Why?'

'Because I reckon I could very easily go as your *Copacabana* Tony the bartender in this get-up.'

Emma spun him around and pushed him back into the cubicle. 'Take it off. Now!'

He peeped back through the curtains, one eyebrow raised skyward. 'Jeez, Em. You should watch who you talk like that to. A guy could get ideas.'

'Well, you go right ahead.'

She had no idea where that comment had come from, but Harry's look didn't falter. He didn't blush, or grin, or break eye-contact. He just looked at her, with that dawning of something different in his expression, as if he was actually meeting her for the first time, and quite liking what he was seeing.

Big brave Emma looked away first. She turned and began riffling through the designer T-shirts on the table behind her. 'Stay. I'll bring you something more you, okay?'

'I'll be right here waiting,' he promised, and it was all Emma could do to keep her back to him and not check the expression on his face to see if that was as much of an invitation as it sounded.

After about forty minutes of shopping, carrying bags full of new clothes, all of which both Emma and Harry had approved, they ended up at the Prahran end of Chapel Street, the electronics shops end of Chapel Street, and Harry was in boy heaven.

'We have ten minutes to get me back to work,' Emma warned.

'Okay! Okay! But come on! I've been a good boy. I've bought new clothes. I've bought new shoes. I've even bought hair…stuff. But I have also been living in the middle of nowhere for a year. Let me play.'

An idea which had been burgeoning in Emma's head for the last hour came to light. 'Fine,' she said and dragged him back into the electronics store in which he had spent the most time drooling.

'My bike is back the other way,' he said, but he did not pull against her.

'Let me do the talking, all right?' she ordered.

Emma walked up to the only guy in the place who wasn't busy with a customer. 'Hi,' she said with a big smile. 'I would like to buy one of those personal organiser thingies in the cabinet over there.'

The sales guy opened the cabinet *over there* and took out the electronic gadget in question. Emma wheeled and dealed until it was a price she could live with while Harry looked on in amazed confusion. She brought out her brand new credit card, which she had only just received, and which had never been used as it was only for emergencies. This was an emergency. Putting a serious smile on Harry's face, drawing him out of his secret black mood, was more important to her than anything else.

'What on earth do you need one of those things for?' Harry asked when the guy went out the back to get a fresh box.

'I don't,' she whispered back. 'But you do.'

Harry leapt away as though he had been burned. 'You are not buying that for me.'

Emma reached for the lapel of his jacket, dragging him close enough that she could feel his breath tickling at her fringe.

'Em?' he queried on a confused sigh.

She whipped open one side of his jacket, reached into his inner pocket and pulled out the mess of note papers.

'See this,' she said, holding them up to his nose until he became cross-eyed staring at them. She then grabbed the new organiser which the guy had brought from out the back and said, 'From now on all of those go in here. Get it?'

Harry took the organiser and stared at it. Then he stared at her. Then at the organiser again.

'You can download almost any game in existence on to it, mate,' the guy behind the counter said with a knowing smile.

'Well, if it plays games then I'm taking it!' Harry joked, but Emma could tell he was still flabbergasted.

'If you get another one for your girlfriend too, you can even play against each other.'

'Don't push your luck,' Emma told the guy with a smile.

Harry came back down to earth and, with a shake of his head, reached for his wallet. 'Emma, don't be ridiculous. Let me pay for it.'

'No way, buddy. This is my treat.'

'Emma,' he said, his voice an insistent whisper, 'you have no idea how much money I have made in the last year.'

'You have no idea how much money I make either, so forget about it. Let me do this for you. It will make me *happy*.'

She'd said the magic words. Harry backed down. 'Okay. But this is not the end of this. When you least expect it I will pay you back for this.'

Pay back. Harry had promised her payback several times already on this visit. Her skin began to flush as she imagined the dozen different ways in which she would happily take payment.

That night as they sat in front of the TV, Harry was embroiled in playing with his new toy.

Emma saw his brow furrow. 'Why don't you just read the instructions?'

'Pfft,' Harry scoffed. 'I am man. Man don't need instructions. Man born with electronics manual imprinted on brain.'

'Then why do you look as though you are pulling a muscle?'

'Because I can't get this stupid thing to work!'

Emma scooted over so she could read the screen too. She

could smell the remnants of his aftershave. The room was warm and cosy compared with the cool night air outside.

'How about you model your new clothes for me, while I figure this thing out?'

Harry leapt from his chair, glad for the reprieve. By reading the manual, it took Emma about half a minute to figure out the note-taking components of the organiser.

Above the quiet sound of the television, with *Notting Hill* playing in the background, she could hear Harry whistling as he played about his room; plastic bags rustled, zips unzipped and dresser drawers opened and closed. He was such easy company. He always had been. In fact he had always made it easy for her to simply be herself. Around him she didn't have to be the good girl daughter, or the diligent employee, or the querulous little sister. She could just be Emma.

She stared into the television. Julia Roberts and Hugh Grant faded away as memories tripped and tumbled across her mind.

One memory came to the fore. When she had first begun to experiment with make-up she had fallen in love with mascara. She had long lashes, top and bottom, and liked the way mascara made her eyes sparkle until Jamie began to say that it made her look perpetually surprised. She had been on the verge of taking his comments to heart when one day Jamie had said as much in front of Harry. Harry, ever her defender, had taken her chin in his hands, turning her head this way and that, as though inspecting her. Then he had given his verdict. 'You have the prettiest eyes on the planet, Em. Don't let anybody tell you different.' Since then she had never worn her eye make-up any other way.

Her love of him was born of a million such small moments, the little things, the intimacies, many of which she

had surely already forgotten. So many times Harry had cajoled her, hugged her, wiped away her tears with hands so
gentle that he wiped away all her grief and fears with them.
But what had she ever done for him?

He finally came strutting out of his bedroom, decked out
in a new olive-green dress shirt, untucked and stiffly resting
over new camel trousers. He was barefoot and his hair was
messed. Funny, for a guy who to all the world seemed as
if he had it all going on, in some ways he was still like a
big kid.

'So whaddoyareckon?' he asked, spinning on the spot.

Emma reckoned that for first time in their long history
together she felt as if she was the one with it all worked
out, she was the one who knew her place in the world.
Harry, with all his natural charm and strength, was floun-
dering and it would be up to her to get him back on track,
whatever it took. Whether it meant giving him her heart, or
if it meant letting him go, sending him away for ever, or
perhaps even taking up a job offer in New York. Tahlia
would say that the wheels were turning, the stars were aligning and everything was coming to a head. She knew that
very soon the time would present itself and she would know
which way was best for him.

'Am I Australia's Hunkiest Bloke, or what?' he asked.

Emma stood and fixed his collar. 'Harry, I promise you
are the hunkiest bloke who has ever graced *my* front door.'

He raised one eyebrow and his mouth turned down at the
corners. 'Em, you've lived here for less than a month. I
would certainly hope I am the only bloke to have graced
your front door.'

She sent him an innocent smile, but decided that was
information he did not need to know.

CHAPTER SEVEN

*MONTHLY **THE WAY WE WERE** NIGHT AT EMMA'S*
'Lovely isn't everything, Hubble,' Keely hollered at the
television. 'You should be with the one who makes you
realise you are more than you think you are.'

IT HAD been more difficult than Harry had imagined it
would be. Sharing a roof. Sharing a bathroom. Sharing milk
over breakfast. Sharing a newspaper, splitting it between
them, he taking the sports pages, Emma taking the fashion
pages, neither of them opting for the always depressing gen-
eral news section.

He had done it before but there had always been a buffer,
a chaperon, with Jamie or her parents on the scene.
Suddenly, with just the two of them, it felt domestic. He
would have expected the routine, the peace and quiet in
which she lived, to feel claustrophobic, but it felt…nice.
Reassuring. Desirable.

Then she had thrown out that saucy little smile the night
before, right when everything had felt extra *normal*, after
snuggling in front of the TV watching a romantic film that
even Harry thought was pretty great.

Then, all of a sudden, she had stood and fixed his collar,
her small fingers unwittingly running along the back of his
neck. Since he had been barefoot and she had been wearing
high-heeled boots, they had been almost face to face. He
had caught a whiff of her perfume, which throughout the
day had fused with the peachy smell of her hair and that

other scent that was purely her, a pretty, youthful mix of sea air and soap.

Then she had given him *that* smile. Little Emma was meant to play with Barbies and sit by the pond near her parents' home sketching the ducks. She wasn't meant to know just how to flash a smile that had a guy's guts twisting in response. He'd slept even less than usual that night, his usual suffocating nightmares a mere backdrop to the memory of her knowing smile.

Now, the next day, on the upper floor of the WWW Designs' lease, they were together again, but thankfully not alone. His team had all happily come up from all around Victoria to help clean out the junk room to make it their new consolidated office space.

The atmosphere was electric. Expectations were high and his little Emma was running the show, making his staff laugh, making sure they were all happy, and comfortable, and included.

He stood back and watched as she chatted with a couple of the guys in his sales team. She wore faded pink sweatpants that clung lovingly to her small frame, new white sneakers that she was happily scuffing in the dusty room and a fresh white T-shirt. Her hair was pulled back into a stubby ponytail. Her face was scrubbed free of make-up, her cheeks glowed pink from the heat of the uncooled room. At that moment, lacking in all efforts at sophistication, Harry really saw the differences in her for the first time.

There was more to her than new clothes and a new haircut. Her cheeks were thinner, showcasing elegant cheekbones that needed no highlights. Her figure had filled out, adorable curves arching just right beneath the thin fabric of her well-worn clothes. Along with this new outer maturity, she was infinitely more confident as well. She handled the group with finesse, with ease, and with grace. When he hadn't been looking she had grown into a truly remarkable woman.

It twisted inside of him that other people, other friends, other men had been on the scene to witness this transformation while he had been flitting all over the country, never in one place for too long, never long enough to form any lasting attachments, never making sure this one attachment survived and flourished. Just assuming that it always would. Though he didn't deserve it, even without nourishment his attachment to her was a for ever one. Unavoidable. Historical. Necessary to his very identity.

As though she could feel his eyes on her, she looked over to him, blew a strand of blonde fringe from her face and smiled, her bottomless blue eyes gleaming in the low light. A strange sort of tightness clenched him through the middle.

'What's up?' she called out across the room, her sweet head tipped to one side.

'Nothing much,' Harry lied. 'Where do you want me now?'

Raquel, in her power suit and high heels, piped up, 'You, my dear young man, can begin by taking me to breakfast while this lot get this place sorted. I am embarrassed you have even seen it before it's ready.'

Harry blinked. 'You want me to eat pancakes while these guys work?'

'Well...of course.'

Harry looked to Emma, who was busy removing dust sheets and ignoring his conversation with her boss. He was ready to tear Raquel apart, but he sensed Emma would not appreciate his knight in shining armour act so he bit his tongue.

'Thanks, Raquel. Maybe another time. When this place is ready and when we can all get together.'

'Oh,' Raquel demurred, backing out of the dusty room quick smart. 'Right. Well, I have plenty to keep me busy this morning so I'll check on you lot later.'

She skittered away and down the lift like a rat jumping ship. Harry hadn't taken to the woman one bit. She just didn't ring true. He wondered if Emma's ploy to help save the company would do as much good as she'd hoped. *Harold's House* would go on whether it was in a city building or a basement or a high school gymnasium. It had been an easy favour for him to bestow as it simply wouldn't matter. He wondered whether Emma's favour had been just as easy. Perhaps he *was* the only man who had graced her door… He walked towards her, drawn to her.

'You could have gone, you know,' Emma said as he neared. 'You are a client, after all. You don't have to stay and do the grunt work.'

'What if I want to stay?'

She shot him a suspicious look from beneath her glorious lashes. She should have known he only wanted to be where she was. Why else would he have come to town? Why else would he have agreed to her cry for help? Why else would he have come up with her name when searching for a *fiancée*? If she didn't know why…then she was in the same boat he was. Completely out to sea.

'Then stop standing there,' she finally said. 'Use those muscles for something other than attracting girls on the beach.'

Hmm. He kind of liked that. He was used to Emma telling him what a doofus he was, not building him up. Funny, it made him feel like a lifeguard at the pool, all manly and protective. He had the urge to wrap his muscles about her and lay a big kiss on that bare neck of hers.

Surrounded by people, he suddenly felt reckless, knowing there was no way he would act on his burgeoning instincts at her place, alone at night. But here, in the fun, heady atmosphere among his friends and colleagues and hers, it was a whole different matter.

During the day spent tidying, dusting, vacuum cleaning, tossing rubbish, he teased, joked, cajoled and even flirted. He noticed how rapidly she reacted—grinning, laughing, flirting right on back. Interesting.

She made him feel so good about himself. Worthy. Fit to succeed. Allowed to smile. It was a feeling he could get used to. But to what end? Would spending more time with this bundle of enthusiasm and generosity mean that her spirit would rub off on him? Would being with her more often, doing everything in his power to make her feel as good about herself as well, make up for what he had taken away from her all those years before?

After a day of thinking in circles, Harry was exhausted and he was overjoyed when she suggested that as soon as the place was cleaned up they could all finish up early. As soon as he trudged back into her snug little home he fell into bed and napped for a couple of hours before he had to dress up for the party, ready to impress her friends as much as she had impressed his.

Later that night Harry and Emma stood outside Lachlan and Keely's apartment. The sounds spilling from inside showed the party was in full swing.

'Are you ready for this?' Emma asked, hitching her sparkly silver off-the-shoulder top up to a more modest level, while tugging her tight hipster jeans lower.

'More ready than you are, by the looks of it.' Harry knocked then grabbed a hold of her tugging hands. 'Stop fidgeting. You look a million bucks.'

Emma did as she was told. Though it was comments like that, which Harry had been dropping ever since she had walked into the lounge that evening, that had her feeling self-conscious in the first place. Added to that, he wore the new outfit she had picked out for him—the crisp olive-green dress shirt that brought out the green in his eyes, and the smart tailored camel trousers that showcased the magnificence of his posterior—and it had her in a spin. He looked too beautiful for words.

Keely opened the door and enveloped them in big hugs. 'Well, if it isn't the happy couple.'

Tucked into Harry's side for protection against the seething crowd, Emma made her way through the room to find Raquel had cornered Keely's man on the balcony, Chrystal was dancing up a storm all by herself in the middle of the room, and the caterers were doing a round with plates of goodies.

Tahlia and Keely sent Harry out to rescue Lachlan. On the way, Chrystal grabbed Harry's hand and wound her way around him. Emma heard his kind rebuke.

'Sorry, sweetheart. This guy doesn't dance.' He then extricated himself with a dextrous grace that hinted otherwise, and made his way over to Lachlan.

'Hi,' Emma said, looking to each of the taller women.

'Hi,' they returned in unison.

'What's up?' Emma saw the look that shot between them and became wary. 'What's going on?'

'We are concerned about you,' Tahlia finally admitted.

Emma crossed her arms. 'What exactly is your concern?'

'It's Harry…' Keely said, her voice a low whisper.

'You can't possibly tell me you have anything bad to say about him!'

The girls all turned to watch Harry, who already had Lachlan and half a dozen other guys in stitches with some wild story. His eyes were bright, his movements lithe, his charm captivating. He looked every bit the perfect fiancé.

'Oh, we like him,' Keely said.

Tahlia nodded slowly. 'I think I'm even a bit in love with him myself.' She turned back to face Emma. 'So we can understand why you are so totally under his spell.'

Harry's ears must have been burning. He glanced up at that moment and locked on to Emma, his hazel eyes crinkling at the corners, his mouth widening in a smile. His eyebrows lifted in question and Emma just smiled blankly back. She thought she saw his brow furrow for a moment but then someone tugged him on the arm, dragging him away and out of Emma's sight.

Keely took Emma by both hands, drawing her gaze. 'Em, I know this engagement thing is temporary, and I know you have reasons way bigger than altruism making you help Harry out, but we are seriously concerned that you are only going to get hurt when he moves on again. We kind of agree we should never have encouraged you to go through with all of this.'

Emma bit at her bottom lip. 'I can't get hurt. I *know* this is temporary. I *know* he'll be gone again in a few days. I am prepared for that.'

'But you also think this is your big chance to show him what he's missing,' Tahlia said, hitting the nail dead on the head.

'And now he's moving into the building,' Keely said, her voice rising in disbelief. 'He's going to be based upstairs? He's going to be working with WWW Designs?'

'Mm-hmm.'

'It all feels too cosy, Em. Too close for comfort. Especially since the whole deal is based on a fallacy on top of a fallacy. He's not really your fiancé and he has no idea how in love with him you are. We are both fairly terrified that you are setting yourself up for the fall of all falls.'

Suddenly Emma was taken around the waist by two strong hands. She bent from the waist and squealed. 'Harry, what the hell are you doing?'

'I am keeping you honest. Why? Were you gals talking about me?'

He looked around and Emma knew that Keely and Tahlia's faces would be beet red.

'You were!' Harry said. 'God, you women are gossips! I promise you, everything she said was true.' He gave them a big wink. 'Now, I need to borrow my little fiancée away for a few moments, if you don't mind.'

Keely managed to collect herself first. 'Just don't keep her too long. We expect to have her back all to ourselves very soon.'

His eyes narrowed and Emma was afraid the words had hit their mark. But then he grinned, his smile so crooked and endearing that she knew Tahlia's blush was more from a bit of a crush than any sort of embarrassment at being found out.

'What was that all about?' Harry asked as he whisked her out to the privacy of the now empty balcony and closed the door.

Emma fluffed a hand across her face. 'Nothing. Just girly stuff.'

'Hmm. That's what women always say when they don't want their men folk to know what's really going on.'

Emma shrugged; he could make of that what he would. 'So what did you want?'

This time it was his turn to shrug. 'I don't know. I just wanted a bit of peace and quiet from the rabble.'

Emma glanced over her shoulder to find Keely pulling out an armful of board games inside. 'They are fabulous, don't you think?' Even though they were sticking their noses into places they couldn't hope to understand, they were doing it because they loved her.

'They are *fabulous*,' Harry agreed, though Emma knew his eyes had not left hers.

'They like you too,' she said.

'That's nice,' he said. Then his hand reached out and he brushed away a strand of hair that the wind had picked up and wafted across her eyes. He slowly dragged it across her forehead and tucked it behind her ear. Emma blinked and her eyes shot to his.

He was looking over her face, over her cropped hair, over her bare shoulders. His hand moved down to rest around the nape of her neck, his warm fingers fitting in the hollow as though carved to fit just there. Then, casual as you please, he bent down and kissed her.

Before she had the chance to think about what was happening, Emma's eyes fluttered closed until the only sensation she had was of his warm lips resting ever so lightly against her own. She could taste the barley from his beer. She could taste sugar from the candied peanuts he had been knocking back. As first kisses went, it was perfect. Light, and delicate, and warm, and shocking and beautiful. Behind her closed eyelids she could see nothing but a burst of pure golden light.

Then his lips were gone. Her eyes fluttered open and she

knew her confusion would be written across her wide blue eyes.

'Just had to give the punters something new to talk about,' he explained.

Emma had no idea what he was talking about. Then, re-membering the door behind her was made of glass, she glanced over her shoulder to find the whole party watching them. Those inside broke out into a muffled but enthusiastic round of applause.

Emma shrank from their encouragement and buried her face into Harry's chest. She could feel the rumble of his laughter but she didn't feel like laughing. She felt like leap-ing off the balcony and putting herself out of her misery. Especially since during every millisecond of that beautiful kiss she had believed it to be real.

'Come on, sunshine,' Harry said, wrapping a loose arm about her slumped shoulders. 'Let's get back to the hordes.'

After a few hours of board games and charades, during which time Harry had snuggled against her, caressing her arm, whispering sweet nothings into her ear and acting the perfect fiancé, Emma was more than ready to escape. Chrystal had been eyeing Harry all night and Emma wanted to get out of there before the girl suggested spin-the-bottle.

'Harry,' Emma whispered, 'do you want to get going?'

'What are you two lovebirds whispering about?' Chrystal asked.

'Impossible to translate,' Harry said. 'So unless you speak lovebird…' He snuggled against Emma and she began to quake.

As though sensing her impending meltdown, Keely clapped her hands together and looked to Tahlia. 'Probably time for the *thing*, don't you think?'

'Sure.' Tahlia smiled at Emma but the smile did not reach her eyes. 'We all pulled together and got you guys an engagement gift.'

'You did?' Emma asked through clenched teeth, sending her friend a million questions with her eyes. 'You really shouldn't have.'

'Mmm, I know. It was Chrystal's idea,' Keely answered, sending back apologies by the bucketful and Emma's panic began to rise.

Chrystal handed over an innocent-looking white envelope to Harry, adding batting eyelashes and a good view of cleavage to the deal.

'Thanks, Chrystal,' Harry said with a wolfish grin.

Emma stepped back and *accidentally* stood on his toes. His resultant 'Ouch!' was music to her ears.

'Won't you open the envelope, honey bunny?' she asked, her voice dripping with saccharine.

'You do the honour, snookums.' He slapped the envelope into her hand and she swore he was hoping to have given her a paper cut.

Her hands shook as she took hold of the lip of the envelope, hoping that Chrystal had not convinced her workmates to get them tickets to a his-and-her strip show, or a voucher for leather underwear. She caught sight of some sort of brochure, and with a swift intake of breath, whipped the offending gift from its haven of safety.

She felt Harry lean in over her shoulder, his warm breath tickling at her hair. 'What is it?' he whispered and she knew he had been as anxious as she was.

The brochure showed a gorgeous old mill tucked into hillside bushland. 'I'm not entirely sure,' Emma said, looking to her friends for explanations.

'We've bought you a night at a romantic hotel in Olinda

in the Dandenong Mountains,' Keely said with a helpless shrug, though Emma caught her friend's half smile before she tucked her tilting lips behind her teeth.

Unable to contain herself, Chrystal leapt in between the pair and, grabbing the brochure, began to point out all the features and benefits. 'Your room has a canopy bed and a working fireplace and a spa built for two. This Friday night the room is all yours. We even paid extra for you to have a late check-out,' Chrystal offered with a wink. 'Is that the best gift you have ever received, or what?'

'Well, it's just about the best gift *I* have ever received,' Harry said for the two of them. 'Thanks, Chrystal. Thanks, everyone. That's really terribly nice of you. Isn't it, baby-cakes?'

Harry shifted Chrystal out of the way and wrapped a stiff arm around Emma's shoulders. He gave her a tight squeeze, which pinched out a smile. 'Thank you. Really. It's been a great party too. But I think we'd better head off. It is a school night and all.'

A titter of laughter wafted about the room and Emma felt her head swimming. She was going away with Harry to a romantic getaway in the beautiful Dandenongs. Again she felt as though things were aligning. Decision time was coming and soon.

'Probably past your baby's bedtime already, right, Keely?' Tahlia said, and everyone else got the point.

One by one they collected their things and filtered out the door. Emma trudged up the line with Harry at her back, his hands resting casually on her hips. When they lifted away to shake Lachlan's hand, Emma all but fainted in relief. She leant into Keely's arms for a goodnight hug.

'Thanks for this, Keely. In anyone else's hands it would have been out of control.'

'No worries, Em. But this is as far as we can help. The rest is up to you. So please, be careful,' Keely whispered in her ear.

Emma squeezed her back, but made no promises.

Later that night Harry knocked on Emma's bedroom door. No sound ensued from within so he slowly opened it. He was more than glad to find her fully dressed, sitting cross-legged on her still made bed. But he didn't go any further inside than her doorway. He looked down at the brochure twisted in her palms and smiled a half smile.

'We are going, aren't we?' he asked.

Emma shrugged. 'I don't see that we have a choice. It's further than I thought this would all go.'

Harry was way beyond that point already. 'Don't sweat it, Em. It'll be great. We can take a leisurely drive up there on the bike. We can go on Puffin' Billy.'

None of it was enough for Emma to crack a smile.

'How long since you've had a break?' he asked.

Her big soulful blue eyes looked back at him.

'How long since you've been out of the city? How long since you have let yourself get away from it all? I would guess it has been months rather than weeks.'

Finally they blinked and he was able to draw himself back out of their bottomless depths.

'That is my forte, remember? Getting away from it all. You showed me *your* Melbourne, now let me show you one of the great places outside of Melbourne. Okay?'

She nodded, her silky blonde hair dislodging from behind her ear and framing her lovely face. He swallowed. Her shadowed expression brought back the memory of their kiss on the balcony, in the moonlight, the realm of the unknown.

The night had been so quiet, with the faraway hum of

cars and people on the street far below adding a kind of magic. He had looked down into his little Emma's face and seen such haunting beauty, such history and such newness all wrapped up in the one charming face and he'd had no choice.

Her lips, moist from a recent sip of red wine had beckoned him and he'd answered their call. He'd been lying when he had told her he had kissed her for the benefit of their expectant guests. That kiss had been for him alone. It had been calling to him ever since she had thrown herself into his arms in her office that first day. Calling to him through the years…

Emma instinctively reached up and tucked her hair back behind her ear and she went from siren back to his innocent little Emma again in an instant. Probably all the better.

He walked the couple of steps into her room and kissed her atop her sweet blonde head. 'Goodnight, Princess.'

'Goodnight, Harry.'

Harry left her to her thoughts, wondering if they were as problematic as his own.

CHAPTER EIGHT

BREAKFAST AT SAMMY'S AT SOUTHBANK
'You think I should tell him how I feel? Satine tried
that and look what happened to her,' Emma said, her
head buried in her hands. 'Em, whether you tell Harry or not,
you are not going to die of consumption!' promised Keely. 'And
haven't I already banned you from watching
Moulin Rouge *alone, late at night, ever again?'*

EMMA was up most of the night perfecting a speech in which she would explain to Harry that they needed to set some boundaries. No footsies and now no kissing, no matter how convincing it might be to those around them. But the next morning she opened Harry's bedroom door to find him gone. He wasn't in bed, he wasn't in the shower, but his personal organiser was open on the kitchen bench. Scrawled upon the screen in Harry's hand was a note saying he had gone for a run on the beach. It was eight in the morning and lightly raining outside. He was avoiding her.

Frustrated to the point of aggravation—at herself, at Harry, at the spinning plates wobbling on the periphery of her vision—Emma trudged off to work. She had barely had time to hang up her coat on the back of her chair before her mobile rang. Thinking it might be Harry, she grabbed the phone. But it was Tahlia.

'What's up, T?' Emma asked, slumping into her chair.

'The Rottweiler wants to see you the millisecond you get in. I bet we are all fired. She's telling you first because she's

117

always liked you better than she likes us. I bet WWW has gone belly up and we will all be out on our butts, and right when that promotion is in the wings.'

Emma took a deep breath and counted to three. Today of all days she didn't know if she had it in her to play fix-it. 'I am not fired,' Emma said, crossing her fingers behind her back. 'WWW is not going belly up. Relax.'

Emma only wished she could take her own advice. Her heart beat so hard she could hear it in her ears. What if Tahlia was right? What if Harry's company coming on board made no difference? What if the lawsuit hanging over Raquel would be too big for the company to survive? Emma felt the cold lick of fear wash down her back.

'Today's horoscope tells otherwise,' Tahlia said.

'Well, you can tell today's horoscope to take a chill pill. I'd better go, she has spies everywhere.'

'Let me know as soon as you get back.'

'Shall do.' Emma rang off, dragged herself out of her chair, then walked the long walk to the Rottweiler's office.

When Penelope paged Raquel to let her know Emma was waiting, Raquel's voice yelled through the phone, 'Send her in now!'

'Did you hear that?' Penelope asked, rubbing her ear as she put the handset back in its cradle.

'Mmm,' Emma said. 'No waiting. That can't be a good sign, right?'

Penelope shrugged. 'Good luck.'

Emma walked in and closed the door behind her. Raquel sat behind her desk, which was covered in a mass of papers. Her glasses were balancing precariously on the end of her thin nose and her hair looked as though she had been tugging at it all morning.

'Ms Radfield,' Raquel said without even looking up.

'Yes, Raquel? What can I do for you?'

'I need more from you with regard to your Harry.'

'More?' She had already uprooted his entire staff. She had already put her heart on the line in agreeing to pose as Harry's fiancée. What more could she possibly give to save her friends' jobs? 'Well,' Emma said, licking her suddenly dry lips, 'what did you have in mind?'

'I want something new. Something big. Something that will put WWW on the world map. Something that will make us unbeatable. Untouchable.'

'*Harold's House* is about as big as it can get, Raquel. I'm sure you know it is the largest search engine in the world used by under eighteens.'

Raquel's eyebrows disappeared beneath her harsh fringe and Emma knew that she'd had no idea. What the woman was doing running such a company, Emma had no idea. The fact gave her chills and she wondered, not for the first time, if all her work might still come to naught.

'That's all well and good, but WWW is undergoing a…transitional phase right now and the launch of something new from the creator of *Harold's House* would go a long way to assisting my part in the transition.'

'You mean to use Harry's talent and reputation entirely for your own peculiar ends?'

Emma knew she sounded shrewish, but she felt twisted and torn and she'd had enough. Harry would be fine. He always landed on his feet. But what more could Raquel want? Or need? WWW Designs' fabulous team produced award-winning work, easy to navigate work, oft-copied work, for some of Australia's top companies. If Raquel only kept her nose clean the business couldn't lose. How could she so suddenly spin the company in the path of that much trouble?

Either way, Raquel had picked the wrong day to be making demands. Emma's spinning plates were a whirling dervish gyrating relentlessly just out of the corner of her eye. She had no time or inclination to add another to the system as she just knew the whole thing would collapse.

Emma stood, hiding her shaking hands behind her back. 'You're talking to the wrong person, Raquel. If you want something new from Harry, talk to Harry.'

Raquel's eyebrows lowered back down to their normal level—low, dark and flat—making her look more like a Rottweiler than usual. 'Can't control your man, after all, eh? I knew you didn't have it in you. A man like that needs a strong woman to keep him in line. Not a poodle.'

That was it! Raquel had finally gone too far. Emma leant her hands on the edge of Raquel's desk and peered at her boss. 'Ever been bitten by a poodle, Raquel? I promise it would not be a pleasant experience.'

'Please—'

'Don't please me, Raquel. I know all about the legal trouble you have landed us all in.'

Raquel's lower jaw all but hit her desk.

'Harry Buchanan is not about to become anybody's *special assignment* so get that out of your head right now. Stop pushing me or I will take Harry away from you as quickly as I gave him to you. Now, I am ahead of schedule on all my accounts and the floor upstairs is all but ready for Harry's people to move in. I thought I might leave early today to get a head start up to the mountains to take you up on your generous engagement gift. If that's all right by you, of course?'

Raquel's face was beet red but she nodded all the same.

Emma shot her one last sweeter-than-ice-cream smile then upped and left.

Sitting at her desk five minutes later, she could not even remember leaving the Rottweiler's office, walking the long hall or even sitting back down in her own chair. All she knew was that her nerve endings were zapping way faster than could be healthy and that her computer was blinking at her, telling her that she had email. She clicked it open.

To: *EmmaR@WWWDesigns.com*
From: *TahliaM@WWWDesigns.com*

So?

So? So. The weight of events finally threatened to squash her into the size of a pancake. She had been pretty busy sending her parents off into the wild blue yonder, working on the biggest campaign of her career in *Flirt*, being offered the job opportunity of a lifetime in New York, doing everything in her power to save her friends' jobs, and trying to keep herself from falling into Harry's solid arms.

All this and Saturday still loomed large. On Saturday everything would come to a head. Saturday was Jamie's anniversary. She had been so swamped she had barely had time to prepare herself, mentally or emotionally. Spent, exhausted, depleted, with nothing left in reserve, Emma typed off an answer.

To: *TahliaM@WWWDesigns.com*
From: *EmmaR@WWWDesigns.com*

T, don't panic. Raquel just wanted to let me know what a great job we have all done on the *Flirt* campaign and as such she has let me leave early. Off to Olinda we go! See you Saturday night.

She sent a quick text message to Harry's mobile phone.

buchanan i'm coming now so you'd better be ready for me

She switched off her computer, turned off her office light and left work early for the second day that week. For a girl who had never taken a sick day in her whole working life that was saying something.

Emma refused to pack little enough for the motorbike to be a viable transport option up the winding Dandenong Mountain roads, so Harry hired a car. Emma would have been happy with a small hatchback, but Harry's idea of a hire car was a two-door sporty convertible with all mod cons.

Once outside of the city she was glad. With the soft top down, Emma soaked in the relaxing sight of tall, thin trees whipping past the car. The edge of the road dipping away into a deep ravine on one side and a steep ascent layered with massive ferns and mossy undergrowth on the other. Even the air seemed green, it was so thick with moisture and warmth.

She slipped off her knee-high boots, rolled up her favourite hipster jeans, so old and stretched she needed a wide plaited belt to keep them decent, braced her feet against the dashboard, and held on as Harry took the corners at the speed limit.

Determined to understand what Harry saw in such behaviour, Emma let the freedom of being a bad girl wash over her, seeping into her stiff limbs, making them loose and warm. For a brief second it felt like heaven, but it was somebody else's heaven. So much of her life was dependent on how everybody else felt.

She twisted her head and watched Harry drive. In his new khaki trousers, grey T-shirt with designer emblem on the front, super-cool sunnies and new beige canvas shoes he looked edible—casual and elegant, but mostly edible.

'What's up?' Harry asked, flicking a glance her way.

'Nothing. Just drinkin' in the country air.'

'If you want *country* air you should come out to Kakadu with me some time. Or up to the rainforests of Far North Queensland. There's this unbelievable cattle station in Western Australia that would blow your mind. The colours of the land are simply unreproducible.'

Emma sat up straight. Was that an invitation? If so... 'Sure. When?'

'Whenever you want.' Harry's flickering glance was faster that time. 'Now, why is it that you haven't come to visit me? You keep whingeing about this being a once a year thing. Why haven't you come looking for me some time? Why haven't you adventured outside of Melbourne to see some of this big brown land of ours?'

Parents to take care of. Work to keep ahead of. Friends to support. Basically, life as she knew it.

Frustration stiffening her limbs again, she pointed. 'There's our turn-off.'

Nearing Belgrave, they turned at the roundabout and headed into the car park for Puffin' Billy, the grand old steam train on which they were to travel out to Lakeside for an afternoon of leisure.

Emma pulled on her boots and scrambled out of the car. Harry's question had rattled her. Why hadn't she come to find him? Because she knew that if she did and he turned her round and sent her home, her secret hopes and dreams would finally be squashed for ever!

Harry uncurled his lanky frame from the low car, hitched his new khakis, locked the doors, then leant on the roof, staring Emma down. 'Are you going to answer me or am I getting the silent treatment for making such a good point?'

Emma leant against the other side of the roof, glaring back. 'Think whatever you need to get you through the night, buddy.' She turned and walked down the winding wooden ramp towards the waiting train.

Harry followed at a trot, tucking her arm into the crook of his when he reached her. 'Now, sweetness, why are you running away from me?'

Emma heard the mockery in his voice and knew he was parroting her own concerns straight back at her. She wriggled her arm free of his and he, being the dextrous boy that he was, wriggled it straight back in again, this time clamping it so tight she couldn't move away without injuring herself.

'I hate you so much,' Emma hissed.

Harry leaned over and planted a kiss on her cheek. 'Nah. You love me to bits.'

Emma could do nothing but growl back. He was just having a laugh and had no idea how right he was. Well, it would serve him right if she was to do everything in her power to convince him otherwise. 'Only as much as you love me to bits,' she spat back.

'Well, then, pumpkin, that is a whole bucketful.'

They walked the rest of the way down to the train in strained silence, Harry happily taking in the quaint scenery around him and Emma seething just below boiling point as they made their way to the ticket window.

The locals were an odd bunch. Slow-talking and easy-

going. There was only five minutes before the train was due
to leave, which had Emma shuffling from one foot to the
other but Harry took to the laid-back pace like a duck to
water, chatting with the ticket seller about the weather, the
journey ahead, the Devonshire tea one could get in the first
class dining-car. Emma had to tug on Harry's sleeve to
make him realise the loud, deafening whistle he was talking
so loudly to be heard over was the steam train's departing
signal.

He slapped her hand away. 'Hold your horses.'

'Hold *your* horses,' she said straight back, which earned
her a confused look from Harry.

'What does that even mean?' he asked.

'Darned if I know,' she said, 'but it was enough to get
your attention. Now come on!'

She hauled him to the platform where the beautiful old
red and black steam train awaited them. They hoofed up on
to the wrought iron stairs and were led through the dining-
car to a pair of bench seats either side of a small wooden
table.

As the train pulled away from the station, it curled around
a rickety wooden bridge. Emma watched through her window as the first dozen carriages navigated the bend. A hun-
dred pairs of legs dangled off the edge of the open-air carriages that resided between the engine carriage and their
dining-car at the rear. When the train trundled off into the
dense rainforest Emma sat back in her seat and looked at
Harry. He was watching her with a hand over his mouth but
she still knew that he was smiling.

'What?' she asked.

'You,' he replied.

'Me *what*?'

'One second I look at you and I see my little Emma,

struggling to free herself from my grip, even though she knows she could never get away unless I let her.'

'And the next second?'

'The next second I barely recognise you. You have changed so much. It's not just this new haircut, or the new apartment, it's something deeper—a strength, a confidence. The way you handled Raquel was a revelation. Did you really threaten to bite her?'

'Theoretically. Isn't that a good thing? Weren't you the one always trying to toughen me up?'

He nodded. 'Now I wonder if you are so tough that you no longer need me to play your big brother.'

Emma bit her lip. The sound of the other dozen or so others in their carriage tinkled in the periphery of her hearing. She leaned in closer. He did the same.

'Harry, I *never* needed you to play my big brother.'

He sat back, his expression closing down as though she had slapped him. 'Em, you know you did. After Jamie—' His throat worked as he swallowed and she wished she could find the words for him. 'If not, then why have you put up with me all of these years?'

She reached out and clasped his hand in hers. The answer to his question was obvious, on the tip of her tongue, crying to be told. But would she? Could she?

'Harry, listen to me. After Jamie went, I was never looking for a replacement. He was my brother. My *only* brother. What I needed, and what I still need, is a friend. You have been my best friend for ever and I hope you will be for ever more.'

He listened. She knew he had really listened but how those words affected him she had no idea. She watched as he slowly but surely disappeared behind the deep hazel and golden flecks in his beautiful eyes and knew that the rest of the trip to Lakeside would be endured in a heavy silence.

An hour later, Harry sent Emma strolling around the lake while he walked to the kiosk for a couple of bottles of water.

His mind buzzed with semantics. The terms 'replacement brother' and 'best friend' flitted through his mind like balls in a pinball machine, slipping easily along his life's pathway until they slammed against a wall of truth which confirmed he wasn't sure that he fitted so easily into either category any more.

Chilled bottles cooling his warm palms, he strolled past families setting up picnic blankets, children riding out on to the lake in paddle boats, up on to the curved wooden bridge where a couple of brothers were fly-fishing out into the still waters.

Emma stood at the other end of the bridge, her elbows leaning against the pale railing, her straight blonde hair flickering in the light breeze. Her short jacket rode up her back, showcasing a stretch of pale skin above the beltline of her faded hipster jeans. They moulded her figure so comfortably it created an ache deep within him. He followed the line of sight of her guarded blue gaze to find her watching three young children playing together.

An older boy had a young girl's teddy bear and was holding it above her head. No matter how high she jumped she couldn't get it but she stubbornly kept on trying. She jumped from the front, jumped from the back, tried to climb the taller boy, even tickled him, in the hope that he would capitulate. Eventually the third of the trio noticed what was happening and he reached out and easily snagged the bear from his friend. He handed it to the little girl, who didn't even thank him; she just clutched her small, fuzzy friend tight and walked away, her head held high.

Emma sniffed beside him. His eyes shot to her but there were no tears in her eyes, just a distant expression. She blinked quickly and he knew she was wiping the foundering web of memories from her mind's eye.

'Paints a familiar picture, don't you think?'

She flinched. She mustn't have even noticed that he had rejoined her.

'Do you still miss him?' Harry asked, knowing his own answer was a profound yes.

Her head tilted to one side and he thought she was about to deny she knew what he meant but then her expression shifted subtly from detached to despondent.

With a little shrug she admitted, 'Every day.' An accepting smile tugged at her mouth. 'Shall we walk?'

He nodded and followed, like a lamb after the little shepherd girl, feeling as if he couldn't make any move without her say so.

'I can't believe tomorrow it will be ten years since we last spoke to him,' she said, her mind once again distant. 'I can still hear his voice in my head as clear as if I've just chatted to him on the phone.'

Harry gave in to the need to wrap an arm about her waist. 'I know, babes.'

'Of course you do. That's why you're here.'

He nodded. But it wasn't entirely true. He came home every year for a week's stay to be with her, to be her rock, to support her during what must have been the hardest portion of her life. But the thought of being on his own at that time every year scared the breath from his lungs. Being on his own at night gave him too much thinking time at the best of times. Being alone on the anniversary of the day

Jamie died would have sent him spinning. Into a panic attack? Into a bar? Into any place where the images of that
day, and the part he had played, could be pushed far, far to
the back of his mind.

'It's not the only reason I'm here,' he found himself saying.

'Oh?'

'I came to spend some quality time with my little princess.'

'Then this is what I don't understand!' she blurted, her
voice rising so quickly it caught Harry totally off guard. It
seemed that their conversation from the train station was not
yet finished. It had been seething inside of her throughout
the whole trip. Her cheeks were even pink. She was upset,
or angry, or embarrassed. He had no clue as to what or why.

'If you miss me that much, as much as I miss you, then
why not visit more? Or better yet, why not return home for
good? Be with those who love you and want to take care
of you. God! You just are so damn clueless!'

When he didn't respond to her outburst she threw up her
hands and stormed off, muttering under her breath, flapping
her arms in the air, appealing to the gods, and leaving Harry
to recover from the unexpected verbal assault.

They had been talking in circles, both bemoaning the fact
that the other didn't visit more, but Harry knew that it was
not in the least part Emma's fault. He had made it abun-
dantly clear that when he was away from Melbourne he was
free like the wind. Whether working incognito on a cattle
station in Queensland, or joining up with a touring group of
Harley Davidson riders through the Northern Territory, it
was hardly the sort of place Emma would feel comfortable
or wanted.

His external reasoning for his long trips was that it all

somehow ended up as part of *Harold's House*. In the last half year his team had added a version called *Outback Riders* using the barely reproducible ambers and grey-greens that one could only find in the outback and the rumbling cacophony of a team of motorbikes heralded each change of page. It had been such a hit with young boys all over the world that the business pages of the top Australian newspapers had heralded it as the main reason for an upturn in international tourism to the Northern Territory.

It was insane. He had had an idea for a nice small business and it had turned into an overnight sensation. He had thought he might dabble in the Internet and suddenly he was a web whizkid. He'd headed away from the cities, kept away from the press, away from people wanting to rub his head for luck, and it had just so happened that his trip had inspired a small adjustment to his popular site and, boom, the economy of the country took an upswing.

The world thought he could do no wrong.

The problem was that Harry knew he didn't deserve a lick of it. It burned so much he had considered pulling the plug, sabotaging the business in some way so that it would all fall apart as surely karma ensured it was meant to do. Knowing his luck, whatever he did next would only be even more popular than *Harold's House*.

The retreating sound of Emma's feet crunching on the gravel as she walked further and further away drew him from his reverie. The one thing that had never come easily to him was his relationship with her. Since she was a kid she had been hard work. Stubborn. Feisty. Opinionated. And stronger than any person he had ever known. Keeping their friendship had been hard work but that had made it all the more worth it.

So no matter how far he travelled, how deep into the

outback, how far from the cities and their long lenses, he always came back to Emma and her life-affirming company. He had considered not even coming once or twice, but as well as feeling like a total heel he knew he would not have the energy to go back out there into the big wide world without gathering that effervescent energy from her.

She inspired him and she brought him back down to earth all at once. She was his muse and his yardstick. She was his greatest fan and his most thorough critic. She was his best friend and…what? She was something infinitely more but he just couldn't figure what it was. The term *soul mate* fluttered at the corner of his thoughts but that was far too complicated an idea to foster.

Knowing he had a lot to make up to her—for having her traipse all over the countryside to keep the magazine off his back, for lying to her workmates about their engagement, and about events that had changed her life for ever ten years before—he followed her at a jog.

'Em, wait up.'

Her footsteps slowed but she didn't turn to face him. He had to walk around until he stood in front of her. Her blue eyes blazed up at him, her cheeks were pink from frustration and exercise. She looked unbelievable. Harry found himself wanting to reach out and touch her just so that he could siphon off even a tenth of her strength.

He reached out to her and she flinched away. *O…kay…*

'Em. Let's call a truce here and now. We're both on edge and understandably so. Tomorrow will be hard but I can't hold it all together for the both of us so let's try to have a nice time. A celebration. We are here, on this beautiful spring day, in the best company imaginable; let's not do or say anything we will later regret. Truce?'

He held out a finger and after a few moments of deep

calming breaths, during which a trillion thoughts flashed across Emma's huge eyes, she acquiesced and linked her finger with his.

'Fine. Truce.'

CHAPTER NINE

GIRLS' NIGHT IN WITH **SATURDAY NIGHT FEVER**
'You're gonna strut?' Tahlia asked John Travolta as he
strutted away from her on Emma's TV screen. 'Well I
want to strut too. Just give me a chance, a reason,
anybody, and I'll be there.'

AFTER the leisurely train trip back to Belgrave, Harry and
Emma drove up the mountain to Olinda, making it there just
after dark. Their hotel, an old converted mill with its crum-
bling façade, gravel pathways and climbing creepers covering the old brick, was quaint and lovely. Harry gathered
their bags from the car whilst Emma checked in. Together
they followed the night manager to their room.

'We have started a fire for you. You just have to top it
up once more before bed and your room will stay snug all
night,' he promised before leaving them alone.

Bed. Singular. A queen-size bed. No couch. The best
thing to do was to make light of it. Harry needed her easy
camaraderie, especially after the odd day they'd had, fraught
with tension and miscommunication and a whole other level
of something he couldn't put his finger on.

'Em, please don't make me sleep on the floor.'

Her eyelids flickered as she computed the situation. 'I'd
let you have the comforter.'

'Em…' he said, then realised she was joking.

'We've slept in the same bed before, Harry. It's no
biggie.'

133

'We were camping. There were eight of us in the tent. You were twelve.'

She shrugged and looked him dead in the eye. 'What? Are you now trying to talk me out of it?'

He had to swallow, her expression was so clear. She was teasing him. This was more like it. This was the Emma he could take any day of the year. Harry reached out and grabbed Emma around the neck and rubbed knots into her soft hair. 'Okay, buddy, you win. We both sleep in the bed.'

'Let go, you numbskull, before I change my mind!'

Harry let go in a flash. Whistling as he worked, he opened up his leather backpack and slapped his pyjama top over his shoulder, ready to lay out his sleepwear for the night before getting ready to go out to dinner, but then Emma yawned such a yawn it looked as though her face would split in two. Harry had noticed the dark smudges under her eyes. She was exhausted and no wonder; the last few days had finally caught up with her.

'Em, how about I run you a bath?'

She shook her head, her straight blonde hair flicking across her tired eyes. 'Nope. You need dinner. I'll just get changed and we can find somewhere…' Mid-sentence, her words were swallowed by an enormous yawn.

Harry smiled. 'Right. That ain't gonna happen.' He took her by the hand and led her into the bathroom. He sat her down on the closed toilet seat, put his pyjama top in her hands for safe keeping while he ran her a bath, complete with bubbles and locally made mango soap. By the time the bath was full, Emma could barely keep her eyes open.

'It's ready, babes,' Harry said. She groaned and held out her arms and for a second Harry thought she was beckoning for him to undress her. He baulked. Stalled. Turned to stone.

'Come on, Harry,' she cried. 'Help me stand up or else I'll be sleeping right here.'

He came back to life in a flash and dragged her from her seat. Once she was balanced on her own two feet he was out of the room before she had the chance to request any more help. 'Take your time,' he said through the closed door. 'I'm going to get changed and watch the news.'

'Okay,' she agreed, her voice far away and tired. Harry sent up a silent prayer that she wouldn't fall asleep in there so that he'd have to fish her out, naked and slick with soapy water. He whipped his T-shirt over his head, hoping it would wipe the ridiculous image out of his head.

Half an hour later Harry lay back against the frilly floral cushions at the end of the bed. The TV was on, but muted. The room was warm enough that he wore his pyjama bottoms and nothing else. He heard the latch of the bathroom door open and looked up. Emma came out with an armful of clothes and wearing his missing pyjama top. The long button-down blue nightshirt came halfway down her thighs. Nevertheless it was the sexiest thing he had ever seen her wear.

'It was the only clean thing in there,' she explained. 'The only thing that didn't smell like wood smoke. Do you mind?'

Harry finally found his voice. 'I'm just glad I didn't leave my pants in there instead or we'd both look pretty ridiculous right now.'

'You look ridiculous most of the time anyway,' Emma said, but he swore he saw a darkening of the cheeks.

He couldn't get over it, over her, with her cheeks pink and her hair tousled from the steam of the bathroom. Her smooth legs glowed pale gold in the low firelight. Her dainty feet with their perfect pink toenails tiptoed through the thick carpet. Her big blue eyes were dark and heavy with fatigue. She was such a vision of feminine glory, all wrapped up in one of his shirts. She had a look of morning after about her that had his mind reeling with forbidden thoughts about her and him. Together.

She folded her clothes neatly atop a wing-chair in the corner then padded over to join him on the bed. She climbed up from the foot of the bed and crawled towards him like a cat on the prowl.

Harry's breath stalled, making him giddy, as if he'd had an overdose of oxygen. When she reached his side, he prepared himself for…anything. But instead of the *anything* he had been expecting, dreading, desiring, Emma leant against him, tucking her head beneath his chin, her soft, warm body melting against him as she very quickly became boneless with sleep. After several moments of solid silence Harry took a breath but since it was filled with the scent of skin and mango soap it only created further havoc deep within him.

What was he thinking? This was Emma. Little Emma. Jamie's little sister. Squirt. The girl he had spent his life teasing to distraction and keeping from harm. He reached up and tucked her hair behind her ear so he could see her face, smooth with sleep; the sleep of the innocent, he was sure. There was no way she would be tucked up against him like this if she had any idea what he was thinking. Imagining. Fantasising.

He mentally chided himself for his folly but the problem was that it was a continuing folly, a folly that had followed him for years. He'd had an eternal crush on this little one. The unstoppable need to tease, to torment, to make her blush, that had developed from the first day he had met her had evolved into a strong, protective instinct once Jamie had no longer been there to protect her himself. But soon, all too soon, that need to look out for her had grown into an affection so deeply ingrained he could not extricate himself from it.

With that came myriad problems. So he had run, far away and further every year, coming back for only a week at a time to fulfil his secret promise to Jamie that he would always be there for her when she needed him most.

He simply didn't understand how he could allow himself to care so deeply for someone—he who knew how delicate and breakable people were, how suddenly they could disappear from life, from his life... How could he care so much for Emma, little Emma who had no idea how her beloved brother's death had been so much his fault? If he had never dared Jamie to take off down the steepest slope of the mountain, he would never have done it. Boys and their stupid dares, their stupid pride. He'd never known anyone with such belief in himself as Jamie.

The nightmare he lived through on a nightly basis came swamping in upon him so suddenly Harry felt as though he was drowning. He was so ashamed that he had pushed Jamie to the edge of his arrogance, pushed him until he had careened off a slippery rock and into a cluster of alpine trees, breaking his young neck instantly. Harry had begun his penance from that moment, by carrying his broken friend's body down the snowy mountain.

He was so ashamed that his life had turned out so well. So ashamed that he was living the charmed life his friend had never had the chance to live. Now his late friend's sister was wrapped in his arms, wearing his clothes, warmed by a crackling fire and starring in his deepest and most heartfelt fantasies.

Well, now it had come to this. He felt it in his bones. This was the moment to prove himself, to prove his own self worth, to prove that he could control his own selfish wishes so that everything would work out for Emma just as she deserved. Her life would be happier, less complicated and more fulfilling with him as a sideline character, not as the main event he had always secretly ached to be.

Harry yawned, the depth of his struggle tiring him. As he too slipped into a warm, enveloping sleep, the one thought keeping him afloat was that he could, should and would resist his feelings for Emma for her own sake.

A knock at the door broke Harry's slumber.

It took him a few moments to remember where he was. Emma's familiar head was cradled against his chest, her small hands softly splayed out upon his naked chest. He moved her away feeling oddly bereft the moment she was no longer wrapped in his arms.

She stirred. 'Harry, don't leave me,' she whispered. The knock came again and her eyes flew open.

'Shh,' Harry insisted. 'Wait here.'

He stood, hitching his pyjama pants to a less obscene level. 'Who is it?' he called when he reached the front door but no answer came.

'Leave the latch closed,' Emma insisted. Harry flicked a glance over his shoulder to find her sitting up, her hair dishevelled, his too large pyjama top lopsided and slipping off, exposing one creamy shoulder. He swallowed down the awareness that was threatening to overwhelm him.

'Keep the chain on when you open the door,' she repeated, her tired voice husky and soft.

'I will.' He dragged unwilling eyes from the view on the bed to the door. Those two words took on new resonance as, leaving the chain in place, he opened the door to find himself face to face with a rather inebriated man in a dishevelled tuxedo and *boutonnière*.

'Can I help you?' Harry asked, his voice booming out deep and defensive.

'Joseph?' the man asked, his eyes squinting and his whole body swaying.

'Not in here, mate,' Harry said.

The man finally realised he was in the wrong place and, without apology, spun around and lolloped away.

'Who was it?' Emma asked, her mouth stretching open into an adorable yawn. She reached up and rubbed her fingers through her hair, tousling it all the more and causing her shirt to rise up, exposing a hint of cleavage between the buttons of her too big shirt.

Harry swallowed and concentrated on the carpet at his feet. 'A wedding party stray,' he said.

'Oh. What time is it?' she asked.

Harry checked his watch. 'After two.'

'Wow. I must have zonked off.'

'We both did.'

Em looked around the room. The TV was still on, as was the overhead light. 'You get the light, I'll get the TV,' she ordered.

The fire kept the room lit and it created a snug sense of romance in the quaint little room.

Emma reached out and patted the expanse of bed beside her. 'Come back to bed, Harry.'

He swore beneath his breath. The girl was so wholly unaware of his turmoil and she sure wasn't making his chivalrous behaviour easy for him. When he paused she saw it. Her eyes narrowed and he knew she was now fully awake and aware. He swore under his breath again.

'What's wrong, Harry?' she asked, her tone low and suggestive. She didn't mean what her body was suggesting. She was teasing him, of that he was sure. Maybe what she needed was a taste of what she was offering. Once she knew she had pushed too far surely that would shut her up.

He sauntered over to the bed and sat next to her, his eyes never leaving hers, waiting for the moment when she would crack and break into laughter, clutching her pained stomach as she always had when she fell apart with laughter as a kid.

But the moment did not come.

So he took her chin in his hand. He looked her dead in the eye, letting every hot thought rise to the surface, letting her read there exactly how he was feeling, how he had been feeling for many years though he had done his best to put space and time between them, knowing she would soon twist from his grasp and make some sort of joke to cover the tension.

But the moment did not come.

She looked right back, her blue eyes dark and glimmering in the low light. Her pupils dilated, her breathing shallowed, and it was all he could do not to forget himself and his promises and take complete advantage of the circumstances in which they had found themselves. She licked her lips and a primal growl rose up from deep within him.

'Em,' he warned.

'Harry,' she said back, her voice deep with longing.

She looked upon him as though he hung the moon and stars. How was a guy to resist? Harry felt an abyss appear at his toes. There was only so much a guy could do to rail against such a force. So, just in case he was imagining the whole thing, he decided to let her know exactly where her actions would lead her if she wasn't careful.

'Em, I want to kiss you so much right now.' He expected her to laugh and raise an eyebrow in disbelief.

But again the moment did not come.

Emma blinked. Had he really said what she thought he had said? It was late at night, they were in a faraway magical place; maybe she was still asleep and it was all a dream. Well, if it was, she sure wasn't going to be the one to put a stop to it. This was a dream she planned to see through to its conclusion. The spinning plates slowed and stopped. This was the moment she had been waiting for. The next move was up to her.

'So kiss me,' she said, having no idea where her sudden confidence had come from. Perhaps it was from his words, perhaps it was from his hand burying itself in her hair, or perhaps it was from the look in his eyes, a look that spoke of confusion and desire raging behind his fierce determination to protect her above all else.

Harry faltered. After all of his manly bluster of the last few moments, he finally baulked. 'Em, think about what you are saying. What reason do I have to kiss you? I have no party full of doubtful friends and co-workers to impress.'

'You could try impressing me.'

He looked shell-shocked. So, since it became obvious that he would not make the first move, Emma took it upon herself. If she was looking for the perfect moment to show Harry exactly how she felt, this was it. Without further ado, Emma leaned over and kissed the love of her life.

Harry's lips froze and his breath heaved in on a great stunned sigh. Emma could not give in. She tilted her head and tried again. This time there would be no room for surprise. She leant in slowly, achingly slowly, giving him every chance to pull away, but when her lips finally met his, he did no such thing. His beautiful, warm mouth met hers, opened up to her, and kissed her back.

Emma felt instantly drugged by the overwhelming sensations rocketing through her body. His kiss was deep, it was devastating, and it penetrated her soul. Her whole body hummed, lit from within by Harry's matching need.

A log on the fire split and cracked; Emma imagined the wood breaking and settling into a more comfortable position and she did the same. Shifting her weight, she lay back on the bed, her persuasive hand drawing Harry with her, though this time she knew he needed no encouragement.

Dressed as he was in nothing but thin cotton pyjama pants, there was no doubt that Harry had become as carried away in the moment as she had. He desired her. Harry, her Harry, the man she had looked to as the greatest man of her acquaintance, the man whom she thought the most handsome, the most kind and the most desirable she had ever known hungered for her too.

Emma needed a breath. Several, in fact. Pulling away and resting her cheek against his, Emma took Harry's hand and brought it to the top button of her shirt. His fingers wound around the button and began to pull it through the soft, oft-used buttonhole.

Emma couldn't stand the suspense. 'Hurry, Harry,' she whispered against his ear. Harry's hand stopped. Emma dropped her heavy head so she could look him in the eye. 'Harry?'

'Em, what are we doing?' he whispered.

Emma heard the torment in his voice and she understood it. 'Harry, please, I want this.'

'Em, once we go down this path, there is no going back.'

'What path is that?'

'This,' he said, his hand running down her arm then back up into her hair. Emma was almost lost to the sensation.

'Making love?' Emma finished, because that was what it was for her—showing the man she loved how she felt in the most intimate, important way possible.

She reached up, ran her fingers through his too-long hair until they tucked in tight at his nape. Looking deep into his eyes, Emma once more placed his hand on her top button, only this time she helped him snap it open. The feeling of the plastic disc sliding through the hole sent shivers through Emma's body, shivers which Harry must have understood as he no longer tried to hold back.

With a groan pulsating with longing and released emotion, Harry kissed her, pressing against her so that she leant back against the cushions, and this time his lovely large hands wasted no time in unwrapping her willing body from the confines of his shirt until she lay beneath him, sublimely naked.

But Emma was soon lost to sensation as she gave as she accepted, with care and indulgence and without restraint. She worshipped Harry's body and he hers, somehow instinctively knowing exactly what would please him. She had never felt more alive. Harry's radiant vitality electrified her veins, rendering her skin white-hot, while the love she felt for him warmed her all the more brilliantly from within.

Minutes, hours, an aching eternity later, Harry lay beside her, holding up his length on the strength of one arm, his hungry eyes devouring her from the tip of her blonde head to her curling toes and where she should have felt embarrassed, where she could have felt exposed, instead she felt cherished.

'Emma,' he said, 'my little princess, you are so very beautiful.'

Emma's whole body thrummed as Harry, her Harry, spoke the words of a lover. Not a best friend, not a protector, but a lover.

He swallowed, the pulse in the base of his throat beating hard. 'I never knew. I never really believed...'

Emma reached up and ran a finger along his trembling lips, quieting his tumble of words. 'Believe, Harry. Believe.'

She slid her hand across his cheek, below his ear and into the curls of hair at his neck, drawing his beautiful lips back where they belonged. She tasted tears, warm salty tears, but too caught up in the beauty of the moment it never once mattered to her if they were hers or his.

As Emma drifted to sleep hours later, replete, happier than she ever remembered being in her whole life, she couldn't for the life of her remember why she had not given in to her feelings sooner.

Saturday dawned. The anniversary. Ten years since Jamie's accident.

Harry looked himself in the bathroom mirror. Some days he barely recognised himself. He liked those days, when his face was wrinkled from too much sun, his chin and cheeks were hidden by stubble, the creases around his eyes were caked in the red dirt of the outback. When he looked older than his years—wise, yet unknowable—he liked himself then.

But the days like this, when he was freshly shaved and clean, clear-eyed and alert, those were the days when he recognised himself all too well. He looked so like the young smiling boy from the photos with his best mate Jamie. Photos from the senior formal. Arms wrapped about one another, wearing the grins of recent victory at the footy grand final. Photos taken when camping with the whole

Radfield clan. Christmases. Birthdays. The surrogate son with the happiest family he had ever met. Until that day ten years before, when Jamie had convinced him to ditch university for the day so they could have one last day of fun before the snow melted from the mountains.

Harry ran a finger down his cheek. So there were a few more wrinkles, a couple of new scars, a heck of a lot of new memories. But Jamie would age no more. No more scars. No more wrinkles. No more smile lines around his eyes. No more memories.

Harry sucked in a long, cool breath through his nose as one blinding memory rendered him weak at the knees. Emma.

He gripped a hold of the bathroom basin as he shot a glance at the closed door. She was lying out there, wrapped up in a bundle of cotton sheets, naked, after a night of being wrapped in nothing but his arms.

What had happened? Why had it happened? How had it happened? Had he finally given in to his latent desires and seduced her? No. She had wanted it as much as he.

He remembered her sweet whispering words. 'Believe,' she had said, but how could he believe that someone like her, someone so sweet and lovely and good and kind, could want him? Had she really meant him to believe that it could happen for them? For real? Was that even possible?

When he had woken he had spent half an hour just watching her sleep, her straight blonde hair splayed beneath her on her pillow. Watching her soft lips, which the night before had quenched a thirst he had not known he had even owned. No matter how much he had wanted to take up where they had left off the night before, relishing in giving one another pleasure, letting her sleep, letting her swim in sweet dreams, meant more to him.

Harry looked back at the mirror. He ran his hands over his face, rubbing life back into his sleepy skin, and was surprised to find no hint of his usual concern, no secret pain, no troubled gaze, merely the remains of a true, honest smile lighting his face.

Emma stirred. She breathed in deep through her nose and shut her eyes even tighter against the thin sunlight streaming through the wooden blinds. She stretched out, her body covering the whole queen-sized bed. She felt energetic, revived. Then she remembered why.

Harry. All night she and Harry…

Her eyes flung open. She stared at the canopy of the bed. The sounds of the morning filtered into her slow-working mind—birds sang in the herb garden, the fire crackled softly in the grate and water ran in the bathroom.

Her hands flew to her face. Her skin felt tight and clean, bare of make-up, washed away by the flow of happy tears. She drew her legs into her torso, wrapping her naked arms about her. Like bees buzzing around a flower open to the morning sun, doubts fluttered into her mind.

What had they done? Had she just experienced a one-night stand with Harry Buchanan of all people? Was Harry in the shower right now, washing her from his body, from his mind? Was that the exact right response? So much for them being best friends for ever. Best friends did not sleep with one another. So what did that make them? Lovers? Or would it make them strangers?

The water stopped and Emma pulled the sheets around her, doing all she could to protect herself from the answers to those horrible hard questions.

The door clicked and Harry came into the room wearing nothing but a towel and singing a Bee Gees classic under his breath. He sauntered over to his bag and grabbed his toothbrush, singing into it as if it was a microphone. He seemed chirpy. Too chirpy. And why not? He was a man. A beautiful man. He had probably had a dozen one-night stands. While he seemed to be feeling high as a kite, Emma felt lower and lower every second that went by.

As his song came to a crescendo he spun on one foot, twirling one and a half times until he faced her. He looked up and noticed Emma was awake. 'Good morning, sunshine,' he said, skipping over to lay a kiss atop her head.

'Harry, about last night…'

'Ah, famous last words!'

'Famous or not, I think we need to put last night into perspective so we can look each other in the eye.'

Harry's gaze swung to hers and locked nice and tight. 'I don't have a problem with that at all. Do you?'

Emma swallowed. She tried to stare right back, but images of their time together swam before her eyes and she had to look away. 'I do.'

Harry sat on the edge of the bed, his towel barely covering his bits. He reached out and cupped Emma's cheek in his hand; it was almost enough to undo her completely. 'Em, seriously, you have nothing to fear from looking me in the eye. Right at this moment, there is nothing I could read in those beautiful blue depths of yours that would bring me back to earth.'

What could she say to that? If he looked at her much longer he would surely see the love spilling from inside of her. But even after their night of lovemaking she couldn't do it.

He was a guy. A guy's guy. A guy who could pull any woman he chose. Emma was nothing special, especially now since she had given a part of herself which he had never known. It was slowly dawning on her how not special that made her. She blinked and looked away as her throat worked despite her best efforts to keep herself together.

'Em?' His voice travelled to her, light and caressing. 'Sweetheart?'

Harry watched her for a few more quiet seconds in which she seemed to shrink before his eyes. Then instinct kicked in and he gathered her into his arms. *What on earth was she so torn up about? Everything was going so well. Last night was…exquisite.*

Emma had given herself to him with such understanding and abundant joy that he had been amazed and moved like nothing had ever moved him before. They had fallen asleep, sated, in one another's arms, limbs wrapped so tight about each other that for the first time in as long as he could remember he had felt as though he was surrounded by a bubble of peace. He felt so strong and so right that for the first night in ten years he had slept without even a hint of the nightmare that always crowded his sleeping moments.

He let her go, holding her at a distance. 'Okay then, Em, about last night…'

Emma cringed and Harry had no idea why. He was re-born. He felt as if the world had lifted from his shoulders. His world was perfect…almost. The fact that he had known exactly what he needed to do to make it so had only made him wish the morning came all the sooner.

'Em, the last thing I want is for you to feel anything bad about last night. Last night was…incredible.' No, not incredible. More. Infinitely more. So much so he couldn't put it into words. He had a new found appreciation towards the romantic words spouted at the end of those movies Emma admired so much.

She sat before him, her luscious body wrapped in a tangled champagne-coloured sheet, her naked shoulders crying out for his touch, her tousled hair evidence of their night together, her tender pink lips beseeching him to take up where they had left off, and her big blue eyes negating all of that, filled as they were with total confusion. She was not just torn; she was convinced that it had been a mistake. He planned to do everything in his not unlimited power over her to convince her otherwise.

'Em, seeing you again this time around has had me thinking about something, something important, and last night was like the clincher, the final proof to me that my idea has merit. More than merit, it has substance.'

Harry shuffled until he was on his knees, facing her, holding both of her hands in his, holding her gaze with every bit of strength of will he had.

'Em, I am asking you, for real this time, marry me.'

Emma's heart stopped. Literally. That was the last surprise it had been able to handle. It gave up the ghost. It refused to make another beat. She pulled her hands from Harry's grasp, gave her chest a hasty thump and off it went again, though by its speed she knew it was doing it out of protest. Harry, her Harry, had just asked her to marry him. She should have said yes before he changed his mind.

If he had asked her five years before, a year before, a month before, she would have. It would have been the happiest moment of her life. But now, after the last few days, after their tormenting kisses, and after last night… He had not declared any sort of romantic feelings for her and that mattered. *Now* that she had experienced glimpses of what a loving life with him might entail, that mattered. She summoned up every ounce of strength she had in her petite frame and took his hands back in hers, making sure she held his gaze as well.

'Why, Harry?'

She saw him swallow. So this was not as lazy a suggestion as she had first thought. Her Harry was thinking deeply.

'Look, we could do it. We could make it work. We are friends and there is no better grounding for a relationship. Your folks adore me, and they would be so happy to see you looked after. And then there was last night. I think we have proven that we are a match in all the ways that count.'

Everything he was saying made sense. Putting the facts together like that, it seemed a sensible idea. Then there was the fact that she had loved Harry since she knew what it meant to be in love. But it simply wasn't enough. Now, after all this time, when it seemed as though her very dreams had come true, she knew that having him by her side did not mean anything if she didn't also have his heart and soul.

She somehow dredged up a kind smile. 'Harry, this isn't Las Vegas. We can't just walk into a church, say our vows, kiss, and be done with it.'

Despite her smiles, Harry's face crumpled. Emma was flabbergasted as to why this suddenly meant so much to him and she couldn't kid herself that it was because of some overnight revelation that he was in fact desperately in love with her. If that was true, surely he would have told her. But had she told him the same? Were they both holding back to save themselves the ultimate rejection?

Keely's marathon wedding planning sessions came back to her. 'You have to complete a Notice of Intended Marriage a month before you may have the ceremony.'

He nodded. 'We'll do that, then.'

He stood and began pacing the room. Emma kept her gaze above his astonishing naked midriff.

'Today,' he continued. 'We can head off now and get it all underway.'

So he hadn't understood her answer. Maybe because she couldn't bring herself to really say it. Was she really telling Harry *no*? Emma stood, dragging her sheet with her, and went to him, taking him by the hand to calm his edgy energy. 'Harry, can you even tell me that you will still be here in a month?'

He swallowed, his eyes finally resting upon hers. 'Well, I've moved my offices into the same building as yours. Doesn't that tell you something?'

'Actually, it does. I noticed in the grand set up that there was no particular space allocated for you on our top floor. No office or desk for the big boss.'

He opened his mouth, ready to refute it, but she saw the realisation flicker in his hazel eyes. 'I never have before. When in town I simply requisition someone else's space.' He tried a cheeky smile on for size but Emma was not fooled.

'Is that what you would do with us? Not create your own space in my life, just edge your way back in with me whenever you happen on by? It's one thing to do that in the workplace, quite another to treat a wife that way.'

Harry threw out his arms in exasperation. 'I thought this was what you wanted. I thought this would make you realise that last night was…important.'

Emma shook her head. It was too much. He was overcompensating… 'Harry, I'm completely without understanding here. I'm trying to be grown-up and think past last night to find out why you have suddenly come to this decision, and for the life of me I cannot. So, Harry, I guess the big question I need to know before we go a second further is: do you love me?'

The hatches threatened to batten down. His jaw clenched but she could tell he was fighting against his nature. He was fighting against holding the world at bay. The cheeky smile would not work here, only honesty.

She took his beautiful face in her hands, revelled in the feel of smooth skin against her warm fingertips. 'Harry, if you really expect me to say yes, you have to tell me how you feel.'

He focused upon her totally, his deep hazel eyes boring into hers, drinking in her thoughts. The world stopped spinning for those few moments as Emma awaited Harry's answer. She could have been pushed over with a feather when he said, 'First tell me you *don't* love me.'

CHAPTER TEN

GIRLS' NIGHT IN WITH **NOTTING HILL**

*'Forget Lachlan,' Keely declared. 'If a guy ever tells me
he wants nothing from me but to love him, whether it's
Andy the waiter or Father Jerry from the radio station,
I tell you what, I'll be his!'*

EMMA stepped back, away from Harry and away from his
on-the-button question, but he grabbed her hands and held
them tight, locking on to her gaze, strong and resilient. She
tried to twist out of his grasp.

'Harry you're hurting me.'

'Then stop fighting me, Em. Stop fighting yourself.'

'Just let…me…go!' She finally twisted away, turning to
rub the blood back into her hands. She sat down on the bed
so that her shaking legs did not have the chance to collapse
beneath her. Her breath came in deep, ragged breaths, gathering nowhere near enough oxygen.

'Come on, Em. I'm not completely blind, you know. I
would hazard a guess that you've had a thing for me for
some time now.'

A thing? she wanted to scream. If only it was something
as trivial as a thing! She felt his weight sink on to the other
side of the bed.

'Jamie used to tease me about it,' Harry said, his voice
coming to her so soft and understanding that she had the
sudden overwhelming desire to bawl her eyes out. 'He
called you my little princess and always joked that I was

153

your prince, slaying dragons before they had the chance to touch you. He was right, too.'

He reached out and tucked a hand beneath the tumble of hair at her neck. She didn't pull away. It felt too right. 'He teased me about it too,' she admitted.

She sensed Harry's smile. 'Of course he did,' he said. 'That was his mission in life; to keep us so wholly immersed in one another we had little chance of finding anybody else even anywhere near as interesting.'

His hand stopped playing with her hair and rested against the back of her neck. Emma turned, hooking her foot beneath her. 'Do you really think so?'

It was Harry's turn to shrug. 'Who knows, Em? Who really knows? Either way, it's what I have always liked to think. That he had and still has a hand in our lives and that we have a burden to do what we can to fulfil whatever promise he saw in us.'

Emma digested Harry's words and, though it pained her to do so, she finally understood the truth behind them. The dawning realisation created a cold ball in the centre of her chest.

'So that's why you come back to see us every year,' she said, her voice flat and even. 'To fulfil some promise you made to Jamie.'

No answer came and Emma took Harry's silence as a resounding *yes*. She tugged the sheet even tighter around her, to ward off the oncoming chill that had gripped her bones. She had never kidded herself that Harry felt for her anything near the depth of feeling she felt for him, but she had put more faith in their friendship than the idea that she was a pity case.

'Well, then, I guess that gets us up to speed. I have a thing for you and you are fulfilling a dead man's wish in looking out for me.' She waited for Harry to say she had misread him, but no denial came.

'Em, you…you haven't answered my…proposal.'

Her head was too congested to think. 'Give me…time. Get dressed. Take our bags to the car. I'm going to have a quick shower and we can talk more on the way back to Melbourne. Okay?'

She tried to stand, then realised that the sheet was hooked under Harry's heavy form. So she ditched her covering and, with as much dignity as she could muster, walked naked into the bathroom and shut the door.

Once there, she spent a good hour cleansing the recent revelations from her body and mind. Soap, bubbles and tears did the trick. Lots of tears. Hot, purifying, bittersweet tears that spoke of the end of an era, the end of her sweet friendship with Harry. As now, no matter what answer she gave, she knew it could never be the same between them again.

Her mind cleared, she met Harry at the car. He looked up at her with a steady smile, but something in her expression wiped the smile from his face. Oh, how she hated that she was about to purposely deny him, but she had no choice. The time had come to let him go.

'Harry,' she said, 'I've been offered a job in New York.'

'You've been offered a job in New York?' he repeated, his voice full of surprise. It was enough to make her bristle.

'Yes. Why is that so hard to believe?'

'No. Uh-uh. You are not hijacking this conversation in that way.' He walked around the car and took her by the hands, forcing her to look him in the eyes. 'Are you telling me that you might be moving to the other side of the world?'

She nodded.

'How long since you have known this news?'

'A few days.'

'Why didn't you tell me sooner?'

She shrugged. 'I don't see how that would make a difference. It's not as though we will see each other any less,
married or not, what with you living in Timbuktu one year
and beyond the black stump the next.'

She could see that he was taking his time to phrase his
questions as the news slowly sank in.

'Are you seriously considering the offer?'

'I am.'

'But why? How? You have such a good thing going here.
I mean you've only lived in this apartment for a couple of
months. You love your job. Your friends are here. And your
family! How would they be without you?'

She could tell he was upset. Using emotional blackmail
just wasn't his style and she could see the moment he realised he had done it too.

'What I mean is, doesn't it seem a waste to have taken
on this great new start for yourself here, with your new
apartment, with no time to enjoy it?'

'Not for a second.' This time she let him figure it out for
himself.

The realisation dawned. 'Because I was coming?'

Emma nodded.

'But why? Why did it matter that you have your own
place for my trip? I've stayed with you at your folks' place
a million times before.'

Emma had had enough of Harry's thick skull. She took
his face between her hands and pulled him so close their
noses almost touched. 'Because I wanted you all to myself,
you great lug!'

She saw the confusion ebb and flow behind his beautiful
hazel eyes. Since he wasn't listening to what she was saying,

she would just have to show him. She pulled him towards her until their lips met in a hard fast kiss. It was a kiss born of frustration and disappointment and the knowledge that this would be the last time she could taste the man she loved—the last time she would feel him melt against her, drink of her, enjoy her, want her.

Her heart beat so fast so soon she almost swooned but she wasn't going to miss this opportunity. She gave him everything in that kiss, every ounce of feeling and loss and even hope. He gave her sensations the likes of which she would never know again. He gave her comfort and desire as he made her feel like the strongest woman and the most inexperienced girl all at once. Finally, after several deep fulfilling moments, Emma pulled away, resting her forehead against his, before all reason left her and she gave in.

'So is that a yes?' he asked, his voice deep and hypnotic.

Here goes, she thought. 'Harry. You were right. Last night was incredible and I have adored you from the moment you walked into my life with that great big red apple. But I will not marry you so that you can fulfil a promise to Jamie. The answer is *no*. Now, we have a big day ahead of us. I think it's time we head back home.'

The drive home to Melbourne was quiet yet fraught with noisy complications. It wasn't as though they could go their separate ways and take the time to lick their wounds. That day they had to visit Jamie's grave.

Emma stared out the window and the land whipping by faded away as she focused on memories of the past ten years. Every year since Jamie's passing, she, Harry and her parents had celebrated Jamie's life. That first year, Harry had decorated the house in balloons and held a great party. All of Jamie's high school and university friends had come, and Harry had produced a slide show of Jamie's more infamous moments. After a year of hard and terrible grief, Harry had helped them all begin to heal overnight.

Other years Harry had taken them on hot air balloon rides, on pony treks, go-cart racing—all pursuits Jamie would have relished—and, though fraught with desperate sadness, those remembrances had never been anything less than a celebration of the life of the young man they all still loved and missed so very deeply.

Even through his busy university period, Harry had always come back to their little family, every Sunday night for roast dinner, bringing with him such light and fun and life that Emma knew he had kept her mother and father sane through those early years. While she had kept their lives in order by running the household, picking up milk before it ran out, organising the bills and school fees so that her father just had to sign the cheques, Harry had kept them happy.

And now her parents had finally let go of their overwhelming grief, let go of their tight hold on the sanctity of this date, so that they could hold on to their love of life instead. This year, the tenth year, somehow it felt like enough, like peace should finally reign.

When the car pulled up outside her apartment block Emma grabbed her overnight bag and hopped out, but Harry didn't even wait for her to turn and say goodbye before he pulled away from the kerb and sped off to take the car back to the hire place and pick up his motorbike.

She didn't blame him. After their amazing night together she had rejected him. What a laugh. She had been the one to finally tear asunder their tenuous need for one another, but his extreme response had only proven to her that it was the right thing to do.

As she trudged up the stairs to her apartment her whole

head felt as if it was full of dust. She showered again and changed into fresh jeans and a black sweater. She wanted, needed everything to feel clean, fresh, neat.

Alone in her quiet apartment, Emma remembered snippets about the day Jamie died. She remembered sitting on the kitchen stool, feeling so far far away and out of the loop, as her mother and father huddled around the phone.

She remembered her folks driving away from the house as half the neighbourhood came over to feed her and make sure she had done her homework. At that stage she'd had no idea what was going on. Just that it was about Jamie. She figured he had been caught doing something not exactly illegal, but outside the bounds of common sense at least.

She remembered the knock on the door later that afternoon. She had run to answer it and opened the door to find Harry, head bowed, shoulders slumped, her parents standing behind him, each with a hand on his shoulder. Before she knew what had happened, she was smothered in a four-way embrace, small and engulfed within the shaking arms of her parents and the slumped form of her Harry. When they were finally able to bring themselves to explain to her what had happened, that Jamie had broken his neck in a snowboarding accident, the main thought running through her smashed psyche was to make sure those who were left behind would all be okay.

Move forward a few years and nothing had changed. In order for Harry to be able to move on, she had to give him up. But so be it. The spinning plates would keep on spinning. Life went on.

She locked up her little apartment and headed downstairs, half prepared to wave down a cab to take her to the cemetery if Harry had in fact gone for good. She was halfway down the concrete path when she saw Harry's bike. He was standing, leaning against it, watching her. The light ocean breeze caught at his hair. He looked so beautiful her feet forgot themselves and she tripped, catching her flat shoes on the pavement. He rose from his seat, but she caught herself in time and kept on walking as though nothing had happened.

His mouth was drawn in a straight line, his cheeks clenched. She knew he was waiting for her to set the tone. She licked her lips, tasting salt in the air.

'Let's do this thing,' she said, grabbing her helmet before she changed her mind. As Harry gunned the engine more than necessary and drove off into the afternoon traffic, she held on to him so tight. She breathed in his warm, comforting scent. She relished the familiar tone of his body within her embrace and she cried. Slow, salty tears trickled down her cheeks before being whisked away by the wind whipping through her helmet. By the time they arrived at the cemetery, there was no trace of them, no trace of her deep sadness as she steeled herself against the riptide of emotions threatening to overwhelm her.

Harry slowed and parked his bike beneath a tree. In silence he took her helmet and latched it with his to his bike. Then, hand in hand, they walked the path to Jamie's grave. Emma was relieved to find their park bench was still there. It was cracked and the paint was peeling. She knew she would be repainting the bench within the week.

Her knees felt weak. She sat. The cracked paint scratched her palms. She dug harder, not caring if it drew blood. The feeling of pain in her fingers helped ease the pain in her heart. Harry stood before her, looking down upon the grass in front of the headstone. His shoulders were slumped and tight. The muscles in his back clenched harder and harder. His legs were stiff and straight. Whatever was going on in his mind, she was not privy to it. But she knew he was hurting. Still. Ten years on and he felt the pain of his best friend's passing as keenly as the day it happened.

It came to her in a flash of realisation; no matter how hurt she was, Emma could not simply leave him be. He seemed so alone. He had always been the rock, making sure she and her family had all they needed. It seemed that none of them had gone far enough in finding out what Harry needed. It was time for Emma to put aside her own fears, her own weaknesses, her own conflicts, and gave Harry the one thing she could. Her love. She stood. Shaking legs carried her to his side.

Harry sensed Emma even before her arm rested around his waist. He reached around her small frame until he enveloped her entirely. His arms wrapped so tightly around her he almost hugged himself. Her head tucked neatly into his chest and the top of her head played against his lips. For how long they just stood there, holding one another he had no idea, but finally the cool of the afternoon breeze managed to seep beneath the warmth of their embrace.

The time had come. The need to spill his guilt, the need for her to know the truth, was too strong to deny. So many confessions had been made in the last few days that he had no choice but to make one more. 'Em, I have to tell you something about the day Jamie died.'

'What's that, Harry?' she asked, her soft, sweet, trusting voice sliding under his defences and making his aching heart all but crumble.

'Em, it was…it's entirely my fault. That day Jamie went down that ski run only because I dared him to. I actually said the words, 'I dare you,' and you know he could never resist that challenge. If it wasn't for me he would still be here today and, no matter how much I have tried over the years, I know there is nothing I can do to make up for that.'

He waited for her tears, her thumping fists, her recriminations, for her friendship to turn to dust. When she opened her mouth to speak he braced himself for the words that he had never wanted to hear. He waited to hear that she never wanted to set eyes on him again.

'Harry,' she said, her voice thick with emotion, 'that is the most ridiculous thing I have ever heard.'

Harry's gaze shot to her face but she was looking steadfastly at his chest.

'Jamie never did anything he didn't want to do,' she continued. 'He was more stubborn than the two of us put together. Without you as his friend he would have jumped off the house roof in a cape, or thrown himself off a waterfall in a barrel or done something equally stupid a heck of a lot sooner. You tempered his impulsiveness, grounded him, and gave him someone else to look out for other than himself.'

Harry's aching heart warmed until he remembered that this was Emma, the girl who wanted nothing more in life than for everyone else to feel happy. Even in the face of his declaration she wanted to make sure he would be okay.

Damn it if he didn't love this woman. In that moment he knew it to be true. He loved her and had for years. He loved her honesty, her strength, her indestructibility even in the face of the most atrocious of experiences. She was the most amazing woman he had ever known, the most amazing woman he would ever know.

Emma finally lifted her head. His breath hitched in his throat as she looked upon him with luminescent blue eyes. 'Harry, I can see what's going on here,' she said.

She knew. Of course she knew. He had never been able to keep anything from her, which was why he had taken himself and his misguided feelings to the other side of the country in the first place.

She let go of him, her hands sneaking up his chest until they rested on his cheeks. Her small, soft, warm, comforting, lovely hands. She swallowed, hard, and he could not have broken eye contact for all the world.

'Harry, you were right earlier. You surely know how much in love with you I am. I have been since I was a kid. But I'm not a kid any more. If you'll have me, then it will be my deepest dream come true. If not, I am going to New York, to start my life afresh, to stop this yearly torture of having you at my side only to spend the next eleven and a half months waiting to see you again. So if your offer to marry me holds, you have to know what you are in for.'

It had taken some effort to get her speech out, of that he was sure. He knew of the torture of being apart from the one person who made you feel…well, who made you feel.

Harry felt as if he was hovering a foot above the ground. It seemed that if he had the strength to ask for it, he was about to get all he ever wanted. The problem was, it was a million times more than he ever deserved.

When he had proposed it had been madness, pure selfish madness. Knowing deep inside how much she looked up to him, he had played on that for his own ends, his own desires, his own happiness. He searched deep down inside himself for the courage to tell her so. But alas he came up dry. Brave, brave little Emma. It only proved she had more strength in her than he could even hope to have.

In another life he would have done all he could to make her his but in this life there was no way he could live up to her towering standards. In this life he would show her his love the only way he knew how.

'That's no way to live,' he said, tucking her swaying

blonde bob behind her ear, and ducking from the response she so ached to hear.

Her body rocked up against his, warm and pliant, and her every fibre beseeched him to give in. 'Then all you need to do is ask me to stay and I will. Ask me to live with you in Melbourne, or travel with you to the far reaches of the country and I will be there. All you have to do is ask.'

He took a deep breath and prepared himself to break her gorgeous heart. 'Em, you were right the first time. I don't deserve this, I don't deserve you, and I never will. You are too wonderful to end up with a dismal, emotionally messed up guy like me. That's exactly why I left in the first place and that's why I *will* leave again.'

As his words seeped into her mind, he saw her face drop and turn the colour of the darkening sky above him.

'You're really leaving again?' She shook her head but he knew it was more an effort to break eye contact than anything else. 'Harry, you make me feel like a spinning top, not knowing quite where I am going to land. You are going to have to illuminate me as to when and why?'

He brought her suddenly cool hands from his face until he held them tightly between his. 'Em, if there was anyone in this world I would want to spend my life with, it's you. But I want you to be free of me. I've been utterly selfish all these years, keeping you bound to me through my sense of duty to your brother and my own desire to keep you close. You should go to New York. You should experience the world without me, without your parents, without this anniversary hanging like a big red mark in your calendar. Your folks had the right idea. It's time we all move on.'

He saw the need to stay and fight and the need to hide away warring inside her. Her hands pulled away and he felt her sinking deep inside herself. Maybe that was what she needed—to toughen up completely. Only then would he be able to free himself of her, if only he knew she would be all right without him. Surely having her ready to take on the world on her own would fulfil his promise to Jamie to help her find happiness. Surely taking her back into his arms and never letting her go would only be spitting in the face of his best friend. Harry bit the inside of his lip so hard he tasted blood.

But it seemed she wasn't done yet. Her big beguiling blue eyes looked upon him, all but daring him to give her the final push, daring him to say something hurtful just so she would go. Her hair hung soft and straight, her breath came in ragged gulps, her nose was pink from the coming evening cool, and her eyes, her beautiful baby blues, entreated him to give in and put them both out of their misery.

'Harry. Tell me that you made love to me last night because I was easy and not because you wanted me as much as I wanted you. Tell me that you dare not live in Melbourne, not because you have some sort of inner wanderlust, but for fear that you will never want to leave. Tell me…tell me that you don't love me and I'll never say a word of this ever again.'

This was it. This was his opportunity to set them free. To give his little Emma wings. To break the tie to her that kept him bound to a time he so desperately wished to put out of his mind.

'Em,' he said, his voice coming out as a horrible rasp. *I must give her this lie, for with it comes her freedom. For both our sakes.* 'I don't love you.'

After the words left his mouth he felt the bitter taste of the lie pool beneath his tongue.

She swayed and he held out his hands to catch her in case she fell. Her mouth worked and one big fat tear ran down her right cheek. She blinked furiously for several moments before turning away. She stooped down and kissed Jamie's headstone, resting her cheek against the cool marble for several seconds, during which time he knew there was silent communion going on between brother and sister. Then she stood and, without looking back, she walked away.

There was nothing he could do but let her go.

CHAPTER ELEVEN

WALKING THROUGH THE COOL QUIET OF A CEMETERY
Emma's tumbling thoughts set down upon the memory of
a movie heroine who had survived much worse. If only she
could unearth in herself a hint of the resilience of shatterproof
Scarlett O'Hara. 'Forget tomorrow,' she said aloud,
'tell me, please, how I get through today.'

EMMA did everything she could to pull herself together before the Australia's Hunkiest Bloke party but her small apartment felt claustrophobic. Harry was simply everywhere. His toothbrush resided next to hers in the bathroom. His scent lingered on his jacket, which hung on the coat rack at the front door. A packet of his favourite cereal had been left out on the kitchen bench.

But Harry hadn't come back to her. The longest two hours of her life had gone by and he still hadn't come home. She could barely lift her hand to wipe away the constant stream of tears much less choose an outfit. So, using the last vestige of strength she could muster, she managed to get herself to Tahlia's doorstep with several outfit selections and a year's supply of make-up from which to create herself into the façade of a smiley, happy person.

Tahlia answered the door wearing an elegant red Chinese bathrobe, green goop all over her face and her chestnut hair in hot rollers.

Desperate to cover up the fact that she was as much a mess on the inside as she must have looked on the outside,

Emma spoke first. 'Tahlia, you can't answer the door look-ing like that. What if I was the man of your dreams come to take you away from all this?'

Tahlia stared at her for several long moments and Emma gritted her teeth and stared back, knowing that her face was red and blotchy and her eyes were rimmed an odd shade of pink. She held her head high, begging Tahlia with her eyes not to ask why. 'Well?'

'Then I would pour you a glass of wine and ask you to wait half an hour while I get ready first.' Tahlia gave her an understanding smile and swung the door open wide so she could traipse in.

Tahlia shut the door. Then, before she saw it coming, Emma was wrapped in a great, comforting hug. Emma hugged her back.

'So, do you want to talk about it?' Tahlia asked, her voice an understanding whisper.

'Nope.'

'As you wish.' Tahlia pulled away and took Emma's bags and led her into the main bedroom, dumping the bags on her bed and pointing the way to the large *en suite* bathroom where she could hide out while she undertook her transfor-mation.

'How does a whopping great glass of red wine sound?'

'It sounds like manna from heaven.'

'More like from a winery out back of the Adelaide Hills, actually. This mask has about another fifteen minutes worth of work to do, so you go ahead and use the bathroom first.'

'Thanks.' Emma leant in and gave her friend a quick hug, as much to thank her for the wine and the company as for the fact that she didn't push to know details about the trou-ble with Harry.

When alone, Emma lay her outfits out on the bed. She

chose a knee-length embroidered silver dress which looked like a coat but actually demanded she wear nothing underneath bar barely there underwear. It cinched at the waist with a matching sash, the V-neck dipping low and the split riding high as she walked. If she needed an outfit to make her feel good about herself, this was the one.

She dressed and headed into the *en suite* bathroom. The well-lit mirror hid none of her recent pain. She looked exhausted, pale and desperately unhappy. With a big deep breath, she scrubbed her face and redid her make-up to make herself look strong and elegant, not as she felt, as if her whole body was held together with silly putty. Just to make sure, she added one last coat of black mascara, to top lashes and bottom.

The eyes looking back at her in the large bathroom mirror looked different. Older. Wiser. Sadder. Tilting her head from one side to the other, she wondered if anybody else would see it too. It wasn't just the night before, the night spent in Harry's sure arms, it was more. It was the unburdening of the feelings she had kept inside for so long. She felt brave. She felt grown-up. She felt released, and with all that she felt drained and done with. How on earth would she get through this night?

Tahlia knocked twice and Emma pulled herself together once more. 'Come in.'

Tahlia entered. 'Wow! You look amazing!'

Emma put on her best party face and spun to face her friend. 'All for the good of the company, right?'

Tahlia washed the green goop from her face, then pinned Emma with a clear stare. 'Stuff the company, Em. Do it for you.'

Stuff the company? Well, well, well.

'T?'

'Yes, Em,' Tahlia said as she shoved a hot roller pin between her teeth.

'Have you ever thought of taking on a position elsewhere?'

Tahlia shook out her ringlets, running sure hands through them, separating them into soft waves. The hot roller pins were replaced with bobby pins as Tahlia tamed her beautiful hair into its usual sophisticated, classic controlled top-knot.

'If the opportunity arose and the timing was right, I would consider it. I hope to stay with WWW Designs for a good long time, but never say never, right?' Tahlia gave Emma a big hug, smiling at her in the bathroom mirror. 'Besides, a workplace is never as important as the people who work there. It's not as though we three need to work together to stay friends, right? Sorry to say it, Em, but no matter if you head off into the wide blue yonder, Keely and I will forever be in your life.'

'But how did you—'

'How did I know about your big job offer in New York?'

Emma could do little but nod.

'Marcie came to me for a reference before even chatting with you. I told her there was no harm in putting out the feelers.'

'But what about—?'

'What about Harry?'

'Will you stop doing that!' Emma insisted, feeling rightly creeped out by Tahlia's perceptiveness.

'You tell me. You can still be who you want to be and love someone else, you know.'

Emma reached over and gave Tahlia a huge hug.

'Hey! Watch the pins!'

Emma pulled away. 'Sorry! Sorry! But no matter what, come what may, we will be friends forever, right?'

'Of course.'

Friends forever. What was more important than forever type friends? Some people were friends for a moment. Others were friends for a reason. Then there were friends one had for a lifetime. Friends like Keely and Tahlia, to whom she could tell anything, with whom she could cry and laugh and look silly and act stupid and make mistakes and watch girly movies, because none of it mattered. All that mattered was that they loved one another no matter what.

Just as it was with Harry. Harry had seen Emma through measles, through braces, through first boyfriends, through good grades and bad, and through the most trying time of her young life—through the loss of her only brother. She had seen Harry through much the same. Their lives were inexorably entwined. Forever linked. Friends forever. They couldn't give one another ultimatums. It made no sense.

Oh, God, she hoped that Harry would one day feel the same way too.

Harry had stayed at Jamie's grave for a long time after Emma had left. There were things to mull over and there were things to say.

The sexual tension that had been there between Emma and him for years had finally boiled over. Yet Harry did not feel satisfied. He wanted more. He wanted not just her lithe body, her soft skin, her eager passion. He wanted her heart. He wanted everything. He had a pretty strong feeling that he'd had it in the palm of his hand and in his excitement he had tried to squeeze too much from it.

'But it's done, mate. I've given her up,' Harry had said, his back resting against the headstone. But even as he said the words out loud, he knew that he was trying to convince himself. The thought of her jet-setting off overseas and out of his life for ever was almost enough to crush him anew.

Then everything became clear.

Her confession.

Her seduction.

The way she said he made her feel.

The way he knew she made him feel.

He leant his head back against the gravestone. 'Jamie. It's now time for my confession to you. I was only trying to make up for my stupidity in some small way. But you know what, mate? I think if I let her go, that will be the biggest mistake of my life. So, my friend, I am only going to hope that I have your blessing because I have no other choice. My life without her is a mere shadow of what it would be with her.'

As he sat there, he waited to hear something—a blessing, a chuckle, anything but the great gaping abyss of silence. He let his tired eyes flutter closed and allowed the memories to fill his mind.

Jamie had loved the fact that he cared for Em. He had joked that the two of them would end up together and, though Harry had always jokingly promised to name their first kid after Jamie, it occurred to him that neither of them had been joking. Not entirely.

It was as though he had given permission without really saying so, knowing one day that the time would come when he would have to admit to the fact for real. But that one day had never come, at least not for Jamie. Had it come for Harry? Was this that day? Was that the promise he had silently made to his friend, to continue to care for his little sister until the end of time, just as they had joked he would?

Harry felt a slap on his back as solid as though it was

real. He sat up with a start and looked around him, but there was nobody there.

He stood, rubbed his hands over his eyes and shook out his jittery limbs. He ran to his motorbike, swept one leg over the seat, donned his helmet and sped away. In the back of his mind he was sure he could hear Jamie's voice, coming to him out of the past, the smile on his face so real Harry could see every ounce of cheekiness as Jamie said: 'Go for it, mate. Sweep Squirt off her feet. I dare you.'

Harry only hoped it wasn't too late.

Australia's Hunkiest Bloke had been announced.

Marcie, the Managing Director of *Flirt* magazine, gave the accolades to a studly young player from the Collingwood Football Club with muscles so big his arms couldn't rest by the sides of his legs. The crowd went wild, women swooned, cameras flashed like crazy and Tahlia noted that an ego to be reckoned with was created right there on the stage.

Emma turned to grab Harry as the winner was a member of his beloved footy team. But Harry wasn't there. Even after the way they had spoken to one another, in the back of her mind she had half expected him to be there for her, to be her date, to make sure she was not alone on this night of nights. But he wasn't.

Emma watched the people on the dance floor, the couples swaying with the beat of a romantic ballad. Rabid Raquel was holed up in one corner, chatting heatedly with a strapping young man in a killer suit. A prospective client? Or perhaps a 'special assignment' of her own? But nevertheless a man so handsome that Keely wouldn't stop nudging Tahlia to go butt in and introduce herself. But Tahlia had a bad vibe about…something and couldn't even bring herself to think about flirting that night.

Emma stuck her spoon deep into her prawn cocktail and licked every ounce of seafood sauce from the spoon.

'So, Emma, have you thought about my little proposition?'

Emma spun in her seat to find Marcie, looking resplendent in an outfit that would have cost more than Emma earned in a month.

'It's been *close* to the forefront of my mind,' Emma said, moving away from the table to talk to her.

'And what say you?' Marcie asked. 'Are you ready to talk?'

Still feeling fragile, Emma baulked. 'If you like, I can have an answer to you by the end of the night.'

'Sure,' Marcie said, 'I'd like that very much. I'll talk to you then.' Then she walked away, the diamonds on her hands still glittering through the crowd long after she disappeared.

Emma slumped back down into her seat.

'So are you leaving us for New York or not?' Keely asked.

'Now how on earth did *you* know about it?' Emma asked.

'Tahlia told me,' Keely said, her face a picture of innocence.

Emma threw her hands out. 'I give up. Maybe I should just leave it to you two to decide it all for me. How much easier would it be? No more decisions. No more surprises—'

'Emma Radfield?'

Emma spun in her seat to find a waiter looking at her expectantly. She sat up straight and held a hand to her heart. 'That's me.'

He placed a plain white envelope upon the table in front of her and then weighted it with a fresh red apple. The waiter offered her a small secret smile then disappeared into the churning crowd.

Keely and Tahlia leaned forward as one, itching for her to open it, but Emma just stared.

An apple.

A red apple.

Harry.

She looked around the crowded room for a sign of him. If the waiter had found her so easily, surely Harry must have pointed her out, but she couldn't see him.

'What's going on, Em?' Tahlia asked. 'Good things cannot possibly come in such plain packaging.'

'I don't know,' Keely enthused, 'it could it be a clue. Like a treasure hunt or a lucky door prize. Don't they usually give away stuff like a year's supply of the magazine or a new car at these things?'

'At what things?' Tahlia scoffed. 'This is hardly a high school fundraiser, Keely.'

'Okay, then perhaps it's a court summons?'

Tahlia turned and blinked blankly at Keely. 'What would be the significance of the apple, then? Do you think Emma might have unknowingly witnessed the murder of Jimmy "The Fruit" Skudeski? I am going to forgive that comment due to your currently crazy hormones.'

Keely couldn't have cared less as she blundered on regardless. 'Then maybe it's a formal offer from Marcie? You know, like the Big Apple. Ooh, that sounds more likely.'

'Why don't we just get Em to open it? Then we can stop all of this guessing.'

But Emma was way ahead of them. She had pulled the double sided paper from the envelope and was staring at it.

The sheet had two columns; one requested details about a bride and the other requested details about a bridegroom. Both columns had been filled out in Harry's strong hand.

'Well,' Keely said, all but bouncing on her seat. 'What is it?'

'It's a Notice of Intended Marriage, for a date set one month from today.'

A long, high whistle escaped Tahlia's pouting lips.

'I bet that would have been my next guess too,' Keely said. Then she realised what it meant. Her hazel eyes grew wide and teary. 'Oh, Em. Oh, sweetheart. Oh, wow. Harry has just proposed. For real. That's what's going on here, isn't it?'

Emma flipped the page. Harry had signed his intentions away in front of a lawyer already. The only spaces left were for Emma's signature and her witness. She nodded. 'That's sure what it looks like to me.'

Tahlia reached across the table and took Emma's hand. Whereas Keely was so caught up in the moment, in the emotions, in the romance, Tahlia knew that Emma was not as surprised and shocked as she ought to have been. 'Em. Are you okay?'

Emma turned to face her friend and she knew that her eyes would be alight with delight. 'More than okay, Tahlia.'

She gave her friend a quick kiss on the cheek then stood, scouting out the crowd for a familiar dark-haired man whose very name made her weak at the knees. But her search was futile. There were too many people, too many dark-haired men, just not the one she wanted.

She found herself suddenly desperate to get a move on, to follow Harry's treasure hunt clue, as surely this was what it was. One of his elaborate plans that only he could concoct. Emma looked back at the form and hastily read the fine print. She shook her head then brandished the paper at her staring friends. 'I can't sign this.'

'Why the heck not? Do you need a pen? Surely I have a pen.' Keely dived into her handbag, pulling out chocolate bar after chocolate bar along with tissues, bobby pins, loz-enges and other paraphernalia. 'Got it!' Finally she held a pen aloft as if it was the Holy Grail. Emma grabbed the pen, but it wasn't enough.

'I need more. I need a witness. I need a Justice of the Peace, a qualified medical practitioner or a member of the Federal Police!'

A bunch of models at the next table peered over at her outburst, but Keely was already on her feet, grabbing Emma by the arm and dragging her across the dance floor. 'Lachlan's a JP. He's your man. Well, he's my man, actu-ally, but I'll let you borrow his writing hand for ten seconds. Lachlan!'

Keely's fiancé turned at the sound of her screeching voice. Before he knew it he had pen in hand scribbling his name and the date below Emma's shaky signature.

When Emma had the signed paper in her hand she turned back out to the crowd.

'So now what?' Keely asked, breathing heavily and en-joying the whole escapade a great deal more than Emma was.

How could Emma enjoy it? She wanted him. She needed him beside her, explaining himself, telling her it was all real and not a hallucination born of eating bad prawns.

She walked over to the railing running around the top of the sunken dance floor. She leant her lower arms on the cool metallic rail and searched the room with her eyes and her heart. *Harry?* she whispered deep inside. *Where are you?*

Suddenly the lights in the grand ballroom faded to black. After several eerie seconds, a huge disco ball lit up in the centre of the ceiling, sending shards of rainbow-coloured dots swirling about the room. The whole crowd was riveted, oohing and ahhing and chattering with delight.

'I don't remember this from the programme,' Keely whispered excitedly.

But Emma stood stock still. Goosebumps crawled over her skin and she counted her breaths as she waited for whatever was coming.

Then, just as everyone thought the show was over, a voice murmured over the public address system. 'Princess, this one's for you.'

Then the music started up. The opening strains were as familiar to Emma as the sound of her own breathing.

Barry Manilow's voice sang from the zillion speakers.

Harry. It was Harry. Playing her favourite song in the whole world. For her.

CHAPTER TWELVE

*GIRLS' NIGHT IN WITH **PRETTY WOMAN***
'It's so simple. He rescues her. She rescues him. And
they live happily ever after. Problem is, I don't think
that I am equipped to rescue anybody,' said Tahlia.
'I can barely keep myself out of trouble,' Keely agreed.
Emma leant her head on Tahlia's shoulder. 'Maybe that's
our problem. Until we are perfectly ready, how can we
possibly hope for our own happy ending?'

EMMA'S eyes whipped about the room, which was pulsating
with throbbing lights and dark, moving bodies. And then
she saw him. Her Harry.

Emma's gaze drank in dark brown sun-kissed hair, an
outback tan, a strong straight nose and clear hazel eyes
dancing with mischief. When Harry smiled at her, her knees,
ankles and elbows all turned to jelly.

She had to pinch herself to make sure she wasn't day-
dreaming again but she knew it was real because her big,
brawny, Aussie bloke was dressed to the hilt in an outfit
straight out of *Copacabana*! He wore the crushed hot-pink
shirt and white trousers she had forced him to try on in
Chapel Street. The shirt sparkled in the disco lighting. The
trousers were so tight they left little to the imagination. His
gorgeous dark hair was slicked back with the sort of gel that
could not be removed with regular everyday shampoo.

Then *he who didn't dance* was dancing, cha-chaing for
all he was worth, his eyes locked, solely, entirely, only on

179

her. Two steps higher than the dance floor, leaning over the railing, she felt like Juliet on her balcony.

The dancing crowd cleared a path. A guy in that sort of get-up was not to be messed with. Harry stopped and held out a hand to her. The whole crowd turned as one to discover the focus of his attention. Emma blushed to her heart's content, knowing that in the flashing lights her pink skin would be the same rainbow splash as everyone else's.

From goodness knew where matching spotlights descended upon the two of them. She had to shield her eyes to see him. His hips still swaying along with her favourite tune, he waggled a couple of fingers her way, beckoning, entreating her to join him.

Without another second's hesitation she did. Like a whirlwind she skirted the railing, leapt over the two steps to the dance floor and hurled herself into his waiting arms. He spun her around and around and she felt like the heroine in the last scene of a dance movie. She felt like Baby in *Dirty Dancing*. She felt like Fran in *Strictly Ballroom*.

Eventually he let her down to the ground. She opened her eyes to find the spotlights gone and the crowd swelling around them, dancing up a storm to the most fabulous song ever written.

'Hi,' he said, the roughness in his voice making her shiver.

'Hi,' she said, not surprised to find her own voice as thick with emotion.

'So what do you think of my new image?'

Emma cocked an eyebrow. 'It's gorgeous.'

'I wore this for you, you know,' he said, a cheeky glint in his eye.

'Well,' she said, winding her arms around his shoulders so that one hand slipped into his gelled hair. She pulled it away, covered in slime. 'You know what else you can do for me?'

Taking her cue, Harry moved so that his body was flush against hers. 'What's that?'

'You can promise never to dress like this ever again.'

Harry threw back his head and laughed, the deep sound reverberating through every inch of her buzzing body. When he looked her in the eye once more his face was still lit with a fever-bright smile. She understood that fever all too well. 'Not manly enough for you?'

'Actually, no,' she admitted. 'I like my men a little rough around the edges.'

'Men? Plural?'

'Well, now that you mention it, I did have a pretty good offer put to me just now.' Emma brought her spare hand around and fanned her face with the offending piece of paper.

Harry's smile faltered. Good. He had put her through the wringer enough to worry a little.

'What did you think of the offer?' he asked.

She looked up at him through coquettish lashes. 'I was going to ask if you were serious, but I know you too well. You'll just threaten to throw me in the punch bowl.'

'And if I said I was? Serious?'

'Well, the thing is, I'm not sure if I am free on that date. I'll have to check my diary.'

He pulled her tight until she had no idea where she ended and he began. 'Well then, you had better make yourself free.'

Her breathing suddenly came hard. It seemed that the teasing time was over. 'Harry…'

'Em, I have been a fool. For a long time I have been running from this.' He swept an arm about, encompassing the pulsating room. 'From the limelight. From success. And from you. You, darling girl, who are the epitome of every-thing good in my life. But you know what?'

Emma could not even form the word. She just waited, sinking deeper and deeper into his sparkling hazel eyes.

'I have finally run full circle. So, Em. Princess. My little one…'

He placed a kiss upon the tip of her nose and if he hadn't been holding her tight she would have dissolved into a tiny puddle on the floor right then and there. His arms slipped from around her and a small groan escaped her lips as he slid down on bended knee.

Emma was so overwhelmed her world threatened to turn black. But she forced herself to pay attention. She had to remember everything about this moment for ever more. The sound of feet thumping on the wooden dance floor in time to the drum beat, the flickering rainbow-coloured lights, the taste of sauce from her recent cocktail. It was all beautiful and delicious and perfect and as soon as Harry smiled his beautiful, crooked, sexy smile she was lost to all sensation bar the feeling he created inside her. No sound, sight or taste permeated her senses.

'Emma Radfield,' he said, his voice coming to her as though they were the only two people in the room. 'I only hope that you will see it in your heart to forgive me for the time it has taken to get to this point. Forgive this simple Aussie bloke. Forgive and marry me. Emma, will you be mine?'

From nowhere he slid an antique diamond ring on to her finger. It fitted perfectly. 'Don't tell me it's your grand-mother's!' she said, gawping inelegantly.

He grinned. 'I wasn't kidding. Her fingers were as fat as

sausages. But it has been resized. And now, if you'll accept it, it's yours.'

A sob wrenched itself from Emma's tight throat as she gave in, slid to her knees and dissolved into his arms. Tears poured down her cheeks, pooling and spreading across Harry's hot-pink shoulder.

After several moments Harry unclenched her hands from around his neck and pulled her away. 'I could always take that as a yes but I would not ever really be sure—'

Emma flapped the piece of paper at him as she took a few moments to gather herself. He stared at the paper, his eyes hungrily running over the words until they fastened on her witnessed signature.

Emma finally found her voice. 'Of course it's yes, Buchanan. I've always been yours. I just had to wait for you to realise that you are also mine.'

Harry grabbed her and kissed her hard, not caring that the legal document in his hand crushed in his strong palm. They kissed like two lovers who had spent way too much time apart. They kissed, sharing tears and little pieces of one another's soul, sealing their lives together.

As the song came to its end, a voice called from above their heads. 'Hey, you two!'

Emma pulled away to find a circle of people watching them. But it was a good circle. A friendly circle.

Harry stood and helped her to her feet.

'So?' Keely asked, her voice an octave too high with all the excitement.

'So what?' Harry asked, wrapping an arm about Emma's waist, his face all innocence.

Emma saw Keely's face drop as she took in his flavour-some outfit. She shook her head, her mouth forming a flab-bergasted O.

Lachlan gave her a little shake. 'What do you reckon, Keely? I can see a whole new wedding theme opening up before us. Disco!'

That was enough to shake Keely from her stupor. Her mouth snapped shut tight. 'Oh, no, Lachlan. Don't even joke about that!'

'Right,' Harry agreed. 'We can hardly have two disco themed weddings in the same social group in the same year, now can we?'

Keely spun back to face the couple in question. 'So-o-o?'

Emma could not hold it in any longer. She was fit to burst from utter happiness. 'Harry and I are getting married.'

Before she knew it, Emma was enveloped in a crush of female arms, the scent of female perfume and the wetness of female tears.

'Em, I am so happy for you,' Tahlia mumbled into Emma's left ear. 'You deserve this, sweetheart, and don't you forget it. Give him your whole beautiful heart and you'll never want for anything more.'

Emma suddenly ached for Tahlia, wishing with all of her might that her beautiful friend could hope to find even half the happiness she had.

'Emma, Emmy, Em,' Keely sniffled into Emma's right ear. 'Isn't it the best feeling in the whole world?'

Emma hugged them back and fought back the tears that threatened to spill yet again. She was going to look a total fright if she wasn't careful. She was representing WWW Designs. But then again, stuff WWW Designs! She gave a great sniff. So what if she looked a fright? Harry, standing a little way away, being congratulated, or perhaps consoled, by Lachlan, was looking at her as if she was the most mesmerising creature he had ever laid eyes on.

She saw him mouth, 'Excuse me,' to Lachlan before he pressed his way through the crowd to be back at her side.

'Dance with me?' he asked.

'Why, Mr Buchanan, that would be an honour.'

Emma grinned at her friends, who smiled and sniffled in turn. Harry twirled her out on the dance floor and swept her into his arms. Once happily ensconced in Harry's embrace, Emma noticed he was tugging at the neckline of his polyester shirt.

'Does it itch?'

He stopped tugging. 'Nah. I was made to wear pink polyester. So let's get this straight, you're saying I can't wear this gear again, even in private?'

'Okay. Maybe we can save the outfit for those intimate nights when Lola and Tony want to come out and play.'

'Now that sounds like a plan. And, speaking of plans, are we going to New York or what?'

Emma blinked. *New York? Oh! New York?*

'If you want that job in New York,' he continued, 'take it. I'll come with you. I'm sure you've noticed that my work is entirely transportable.'

'Sure. I don't know. Maybe.'

Wow, how easily that had all slipped her mind in the last half an hour. Well, as far as she was concerned, it could wait a little while longer yet. Keely was set with Lachlan at her side. Tahlia was happy to take life's changes as they came. Her parents were having a wonderful romantic time snorkelling and scuba-diving. It seemed everyone was all right. Nobody needed to be looked after. It seemed it was her turn to be thoroughly spoilt.

As though sensing her thoughts, Harry reached up and stroked the back of her hair and it felt like the most natural thing in the world for Emma to tuck her head against his shoulder.

'I don't remember a time when I have ever been happier, Buchanan,' Emma said.

'Princess,' Harry nuzzled against her ear. 'This is only the beginning.'

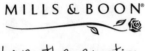

MILLS & BOON®

Live the emotion

AUGUST 2005 HARDBACK TITLES

ROMANCE™

The Brazilian's Blackmailed Bride *Michelle Reid*		
	H6228	0 263 18723 3
Expecting the Playboy's Heir *Penny Jordan*		
	H6229	0 263 18724 1
The Tycoon's Trophy Wife *Miranda Lee*	H6230	0 263 18725 X
Wedding Vow of Revenge *Lucy Monroe*	H6231	0 263 18726 8
Sale or Return Bride *Sarah Morgan*	H6232	0 263 18727 6
Prince's Passion *Carole Mortimer*	H6233	0 263 18728 4
The Mancini Marriage Bargain *Trish Morey*	H6234	0 263 18729 2
The Rich Man's Virgin *Lindsay Armstrong*	H6235	0 263 18730 6
Marriage at Murraree *Margaret Way*	H6236	0 263 18731 4
Winning Back His Wife *Barbara McMahon*	H6237	0 263 18732 2
Just Friends to...Just Married *Renee Roszel*		
	H6238	0 263 18733 0
The Shock Engagement *Ally Blake*	H6239	0 263 18734 9
To Kiss a Sheikh *Teresa Southwick*	H6240	0 263 18735 7
The Boss's Baby Surprise *Lilian Darcy*	H6241	0 263 18736 5
Bride by Accident *Marion Lennox*	H6242	0 263 18737 3
A Surgeon's Marriage Wish *Abigail Gordon*	H6243	0 263 18738 1

HISTORICAL ROMANCE™

The Marriage Debt *Louise Allen*	H606	0 263 18817 5
The Rake and the Rebel *Mary Brendan*	H607	0 263 18818 3
The Engagement *Kate Bridges*	H608	0 263 18948 1

MEDICAL ROMANCE™

Spanish Doctor, Pregnant Nurse *Carol Marinelli*		
	M523	0 263 18841 8
Coming Home to Katoomba *Lucy Clark*	M524	0 263 18842 6

0705 Gen Std HB

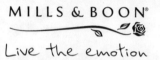

Live the emotion

AUGUST 2005 LARGE PRINT TITLES

ROMANCE™

Possessed by the Sheikh *Penny Jordan*	1791	0 263 18571 0
The Disobedient Bride *Helen Bianchin*	1792	0 263 18572 9
His Pregnant Mistress *Carol Marinelli*	1793	0 263 18573 7
The Future King's Bride *Sharon Kendrick*	1794	0 263 18574 5
Vacancy: Wife of Convenience *Jessica Steele*		
	1795	0 263 18575 3
His Hired Bride *Susan Fox*	1796	0 263 18576 1
In the Shelter of His Arms *Jackie Braun*	1797	0 263 18577 X
The Marriage Adventure *Hannah Bernard*	1798	0 263 18578 8

HISTORICAL ROMANCE™

Her Gentleman Protector *Meg Alexander*	304	0 263 18505 2
A Perfect Knight *Anne Herries*	305	0 263 18506 0
A Wild Justice *Gail Ranstrom*	306	0 263 18954 6

MEDICAL ROMANCE™

Emergency at Inglewood *Alison Roberts*	569	0 263 18471 4
A Very Special Midwife *Gill Sanderson*	570	0 263 18472 2
The GP's Valentine Proposal *Jessica Matthews*		
	571	0 263 18473 0
The Doctors' Baby Bond *Abigail Gordon*	572	0 263 18474 9

0705 Gen Std LP

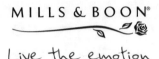

MILLS & BOON®

Live the emotion

SEPTEMBER 2005 HARDBACK TITLES

ROMANCE™

The Disobedient Virgin *Sandra Marton*	H6244	0 263 18739 X
A Scandalous Marriage *Miranda Lee*	H6245	0 263 18740 3
Sleeping with a Stranger *Anne Mather*	H6246	0 263 18741 1
At the Italian's Command *Cathy Williams*	H6247	0 263 18742 X
Prince's Pleasure *Carole Mortimer*	H6248	0 263 18743 8
His One-Night Mistress *Sandra Field*	H6249	0 263 18744 6
The Royal Baby Bargain *Robyn Donald*	H6250	0 263 18745 4
Back in her Husband's Bed *Melanie Milburne*		
	H6251	0 263 18746 2
Wife and Mother Forever *Lucy Gordon*	H6252	0 263 18747 0
Christmas Gift: A Family *Barbara Hannay*		
	H6253	0 263 18748 9
Mistletoe Marriage *Jessica Hart*	H6254	0 263 18749 7
Taking on the Boss *Darcy Maguire*	H6255	0 263 18750 0
To Wed a Sheikh *Teresa Southwick*	H6256	0 263 18751 9
Major Daddy *Cara Colter*	H6257	0 263 18752 7
A Child To Call Her Own *Gill Sanderson*	H6258	0 263 18753 5
Coming Home for Christmas *Meredith Webber*		
	H6259	0 263 18754 3

HISTORICAL ROMANCE™

A Reputable Rake *Diane Gaston*	H609	0 263 18819 1
Conquest Bride *Meriel Fuller*	H610	0 263 18820 5
Princess of Fortune *Miranda Jarrett*	H611	0 263 18949 X

MEDICAL ROMANCE™

The Nurse's Christmas Wish *Sarah Morgan*		
	M525	0 263 18843 4
The Consultant's Christmas Proposal *Kate Hardy*		
	M526	0 263 18844 2

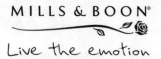

MILLS & BOON®

Live the emotion

SEPTEMBER 2005 LARGE PRINT TITLES

ROMANCE™

The Italian's Stolen Bride *Emma Darcy*	1799	0 263 18579 6	
The Purchased Wife *Michelle Reid*	1800	0 263 18580 X	
Bound by Blackmail *Kate Walker*	1801	0 263 18581 8	
Public Wife, Private Mistress *Sarah Morgan*			
	1802	0 263 18582 6	
Their Pregnancy Bombshell *Barbara McMahon*			
	1803	0 263 18583 4	
The Corporate Marriage Campaign *Leigh Michaels*			
	1804	0 263 18584 2	
A Mother For His Daughter *Ally Blake*	1805	0 263 18585 0	
The Boss's Convenient Bride *Jennie Adams*			
	1806	0 263 18586 9	

HISTORICAL ROMANCE™

A Model Débutante *Louise Allen*	307	0 263 18507 9
The Bought Bride *Juliet Landon*	308	0 263 18508 7
Raven's Vow *Gayle Wilson*	309	0 263 18955 4

MEDICAL ROMANCE™

His Longed-For Baby *Josie Metcalfe*	573	0 263 18475 7
Emergency: A Marriage Worth Keeping *Carol Marinelli*		
	574	0 263 18476 5
The Greek Doctor's Rescue *Meredith Webber*		
	575	0 263 18477 3
The Consultant's Secret Son *Joanna Neil*	576	0 263 18478 1

0805 Gen Std LP